CULTURAL LEARNINGS OF LONDON FOR THE BENEFIT OF SISTER OF THAT KAZAKH REPORTER

Gul Aina

ISBN: 979-8-89686-906-3

CONTENTS

PREFACE

The REAL Kazakhstan: A Guide for Ignorant Westerners

Listen here, you people who think Kazakhstan is just what my stupid brother showed in his movie - let me tell you about REAL Kazakhstan, most glorious country in all of Central Asia (not counting times when Uzbekistan cheats in Olympics).

Our Great Land

Kazakhstan is bigger than Western Europe! While you English people living on tiny island fighting over last parking space in Tesco, we have so much space, sometimes we lose whole village and only find it next spring when snow melts. We stretch from Caspian Sea (which has best sturgeon, even Russian mafia agree) to Altai Mountains, which are like Alps but with better views and less yodeling.

Weather

You think your London weather bad? Ha! In Kazakhstan, we have PROPER weather. Winter so cold it freeze words in your mouth - must wait until spring to finish conversation. Summer so hot, even camels wear sunscreen. But we are strong people - we don't complain about weather like British people who need therapy when sun comes out.

Our Noble Culture

First thing you must know - we did NOT get independence in 1991 because we were "part of Soviet Union." No! We ALLOWED Soviets to think they were in charge while secretly keeping our culture alive. Very clever plan!

Traditional life centered around yurt - which is NOT "tent" like ignorant Western people say. Is engineering masterpiece that can be built faster than IKEA furniture and never loses parts! Try doing that with your fancy London flat!

Our Superior Language

Kazakh language so sophisticated, we need two alphabets just to express all meanings! Not like English where "through," "though," "tough," and "thorough" all look same but mean different things. This is crazy system! Our language make sense - when we say word, you know exactly if we offering you food or challenging you to wrestling match.

Modern Kazakhstan

Things you might not know about MY Kazakhstan:

We have more smartphones per person than London (because our phones actually work!)

Our internet faster than British internet (because we install cables AFTER 1985)

Astana city more modern than your fancy London - our buildings actually MEANT to look like alien spaceships

Things My Stupid Brother Got Wrong:

No, we do NOT keep cows in house (except when is very cold)

Women have ALL rights (including right to tell men they are stupid)

Our scientists very clever - first people to discover that pain in toe can mean problem in head (especially if someone hit you there)

Final Words

Next time you think about Kazakhstan, remember: we are proud nation with history longer than your British monarchy.

We invented apples, pants (probably), and best way to ferment horse milk. While London still arguing about whether to have Olympics, we already teaching eagles to catch drones!

And yes, we have potassium. Very good potassium. But is NOT only thing we have!

> **Note: Any complaints about this guide can be addressed to my brother, who started all this nonsense. I am just trying to fix his mess.**

Sincerely,

Lapshagul (Who is actually successful London businesswoman now, thank you very much!)

CHAPTER 1

Arrived

My brother always say, "Great success come to those who take many risks!" So here I am in London, land of Queen and crumpets, after thirteen-hour flight where I hold my pee like champion weightlifter holds barbell. Why I hold? Because if plane crash, I want dignity in death. No one say, "Here lie Borat's sister, who die with wet pants."

Airplane lady - what you call them, flight attender? - she try feed me Western propaganda food. I ask for shorpo, traditional soup of my people, and she look at me as if I ask for horse testicle. (Which actually very good with salt, but that different story). In Kazakhstan, even smallest village airplane has shorpo. British Airways? Pfft. Only thing you get is tiny whiskey bottle and sense of regret.

At airport, I stand by spinning luggage circle. Two hours I wait! Then I see my bag going round-round on different circle, confusing me like gypsy fortuneteller. My brother warn me about Western trickery, but he not mention luggage that play hide and seek.

Outside airport, I expect to see famous Oxford Street, maybe catch glimpse of Harry Potter flying on broomstick. Instead, only darkness and signs pointing to train stations. London has more train stations than Kazakhstan has potassium, and we are world champion of potassium! I take taxi, say "Knightsbridge Street, please" because my English teacher say British people love word "please" more than they love queuing.

First taxi driver, this clever bastard, he ask if Zhanakorgan in whales. I laugh because how can city be inside fish? Later I realize he make fool of me. He charge five twenty-pound notes, which I give because in Zhanakorgan we are generous people. But I make mental note: when I become famous superstar, I buy his taxi company just to fire him.

Second taxi, I tell driver straight away - you try funny business, I show you torture technique I learn from watching American CIA movies. He laugh, but he take me straight to Harrods like good boy. When he try ask for more money, I threaten to tell police he try inappropriate things. My brother teach me well - best defense is good offense, and second best defense is lawsuit threat.

In Harrods, I ready to show London that Kazakh women do it all – milk horse, catch chicken, break stallion, look sexy in high heels. Very sophisticated. Shop lady stop me from taking bag in changing room, say I might steal "by mistake." How you steal by mistake? In Zhanakorgan, we have saying: "Thief who steal by accident is just stupid person with poor planning."

I drink coffee with African lady who make joke about my brother's friend Ali G. She have ass like prize-winning watermelon, very impressive! I tell her she waste talent making coffee, should be comedian. In my country, with ass like that, she already be minister of agriculture.

You know what? My brother may be famous for making my country look foolish, but I come to London to show different side. I have special power – when I touch things, they grow bigger, better, stronger. Like Kazakhstan's reputation after I finish with this city. Just watch me shine brighter than uranium in government laboratory!

Here I am with my coffee, dragging stupid suitcase down Knightsbridge Street until I find this place called Shepherds Bush. Who names place after shepherd's bush? Back home, we give places proper names, like "City of Glory" or "Mountain of

Dreams," not some farmer's private garden. And trust me, you don't want to see Kazakh shepherd's bush— our shepherds are women built like Soviet tanks and have more hair than the sheep they herd.

But no more bush talk. I must do serious journalism now. With edge. (Still not sure what edge means in English—maybe they want me to write from roof?)

This Shepherds Bush is not what tourist books promise. No fancy London with Big Ben and royal guards in funny hats. Instead, I get crowd of people wearing clothes that look like made from leftover plastic bags, everyone shouting in languages I never knew existed. White English people here look like they fight bears for hobby, but Black people—they scary in good way, like movie stars who could kill you but choose not to.

I drag my bag (now with three wheels because London streets are hungry) to my new house address. Ring bell. Suddenly, big woman head appears from window like surprise puppet show. "Whaddya want?!" she shouts down. She is Black and scary, and I already like her very much.

"Hello-hello! I am Lapshagul!" I call up, neck starting to hurt.

She yells back, "Eh?! Which *gul* you *shag*?! No shagging here on mah doorstep, innit! This honorable house, no prozzies!"

I start to think maybe she makes fun of my name, but before I can explain that Lapshagul means "Lying Flower" in my language (though maybe not so pretty in English), she disappears. Then—bam! —door opens and there she stands, big like mountain and laughing. She pulls me inside while I wonder if I need use my special Kazakh defense moves, but then she says nice things: "Just playing with you, darling! Been expecting you!"

We go upstairs—she has to walk sideways because her bottom is... how to say... very ambitious with space. All time she looks at me with big smile, maybe thinking what kind of trouble I bring to her house. Then she shows me room that is... is... smaller than box where my uncle keeps his prize potatoes. One sad little bed, one lonely chair, that's all.

"Hey Missus," I say, trying to be diplomatic, "agency told me this was penthouse. This not penthouse—this where mouse would complain about property values!"

Her face goes serious like Lenin statue. "Listen here, little Missy, in da Bush, you gets what you given, innit?" Then she laughs again like everything is big joke. I too tired to argue, but maybe I put her name on my special list. (Is list of people who maybe need to find surprise fish in their curtain rods later.)

I am what English people call "totally fucked"—means tired, not other thing—so I just want sleep. Take off clothes, lie on tiny bed. Room is hot like sauna but without nice steam. I so exhausted I forget about curtains, and when I wake up two hours later, I see through window across roof there is naked man watching me and doing something with hands that looks he play dombra, but window too foggy to be sure. Very strange—I not know London men play my country national instrument, but every day is learning experience.

Later, I go look for bath, forget I still naked (in Kazakhstan, family house means no shame). Landlady appears from nowhere, starts screaming: "What you doing, ya crazy bitch?! Can't be showing titties an' pussyclat in my house!" I don't know what is pussyclat, but she smiles while she yells, and her eyes stay too long on parts that apparently need covering in England.

I go back upstairs, no bath today. Right now, stomach say forget bath, forget London culture learning—just need big plate of beshbarmak or will die from hunger. Why nobody here know proper food? Why everything fish with potato? Why life so hard in this strange city?

CHAPTER 2

Revenge

I walk Bush Street, searching for taste of homeland. But what I find? Only endless parade of fried chicken shops and burger places. My stomach make angry noises like constipated yak - very embarrassing in public place. If I don't eat soon, I will become what English people call "hangry beast," which I think is like hungry bear but with worse attitude.

After much walking, I accept sad truth - no Kazakh food in Bush. But! I hear whispers of place called Flying Tyshkan in area named Elephant and Castle. Very strange name - in my country, we give sensible names like "Village Where Goat Ate Mayor's Hat." This Flying Tyshkan could be restaurant or pub house. I nervous about pub houses because last time I visit one, man try to teach me "British dancing" which look suspiciously same as seizure.

Universe has sense of humor - taxi that stops is same one with driver who take me on "scenic route" from airport last week! He charge me enough money to buy small farm in homeland. He not recognize me - maybe think all foreigners look same, like I think all British people look like Queen on money (except some have worse teeth).

I get in back of taxi, say "Elephant and Castle" in my most proper English, which I learn from watching BBC show about angry chef who swear at everyone. Driver's face get smirk wider than cat who find unlocked bird cage. What he not know is I have clever phone now with map app.

Technology is wonderful thing - in my country, no need for GPS, we just follow trail of potato peels. Works 90% of time, except when birds eat GPS system.

This silly man drive in circles bigger than my aunt Svetlana's wedding dress (she marry very rich potato farmer). After watching him make shape that would make geometry teacher cry, I decide to give him taste of own medicine.

"Stop!" I announce with drama of soap opera actress. "Must report crime!"

His eyes get big. "What crime?"

"You try steal my money with fancy driving! Map show truth like mirror show nose hair!"

His face turn color of bad borscht. Driver now sweating like pig in sauna, which I know about because my uncle run combination pig farm and sauna (business not success). He try to make me leave taxi, but I channel spirit of great-grandmother who once wrestle bear for last bottle of vodka.

"Cannot leave!" I declare. "Need compensation for grand tour of London nobody ask for! You think I stupid tourist who not know difference between straight line and pretzel shape?"

He makes many interesting noises; call me words I pretend not understand (but actually know very well from watching British football matches). Finally throw money at me like feeding angry goose. Hundred pounds! In my country, this enough money to buy three goats and small bicycle.

I leave taxi with dignity of victorious warrior, give him traditional gesture of disapproval (yes, middle finger universal language). As I walk away, think maybe London teaching me something - sometimes best revenge is making someone else look like bigger idiot than they think you are.

Now to find this flying restaurant. Hope food not actually

flying - catching dinner in mid-air very difficult, especially after getting manicure.

CHAPTER 3

Mfanni

Finally, like brave explorer finding new continent, I discover Flying Tishkan! I later find out named after owner's crazy Uncle Dimitri who one night get so drunk he launch fat mouse across barn using mama-in-law's fancy panties like magic carpet, and everybody laugh so hard they forget to milk goats!

But first, special mission: pick up my new friend from coffee shop.

And there she is – Mfanni! Beautiful African queen waiting for me as if we plan this meeting for hundred years.

She kiss my forehead so hard, I think maybe her lips have special African superglue. Like octopus trying to eat small fish, but with more lipstick. After we finally unstick (took some effort, let me tell you), she start talking about spiritual connections and destiny. I get little nervous – in Zhanakorgan, when someone talk about destiny, they usually try to sell you magic beans or arrange marriage.

But my stomach making angry revolution noises, and when stomach angry, brain cannot think straight. This is scientific fact from University of Zhanakorgan (which maybe exist, maybe not).

Inside Flying Tishkan, heaven open up! Real zhaya! Actual beshbarmak! But something smell fishy – and not just food. Waiters about as Kazakh as Queen of England. Main waiter-man call himself Arsen (ha! And I am Queen of Mars). He is Russian trying to be Kazakh, like wolf wearing sheep costume but forgetting to hide vodka breath.

This fake-Kazakh Arsen (probably real name Vladimir or Boris or Maybe- I-Think-I-Fool-Everyone) give me look like I am KGB spy. So, I do what any smart Kazakh woman do – I speak proper Kazakh to him. His face become confused like goat trying to solve mathematics. He slide away, probably to tell other fake-Kazakhs that I catch his little performance.

"What happening?" Mfanni ask, watching drama unfold like soap opera.

"He is Russian kynap," I explain. She not ask what kynap mean. Smart girl – some words better left mysterious.

While we stuff faces with homeland cooking (my tears of joy make food extra salty), I ask Mfanni about coffee shop job.

"So why you work there? You look like woman who should be running nightclub, not serving lattes to tourists."

She snorts. "I used to, you know. Not a nightclub, but something close. Back home in Kingston."

I raise eyebrow, wiping beshbarmak sauce from lips. "Kingston? The reggae place?"

Mfanni leans back, tapping her nails against glass. "Yeah, girl. The reggae place. I was running little bar with my cousin, real good money. We had live music, proper DJs, place packed every night. Then one night—BOOM! —trouble walks in. Some big-shot gangster decide he own the place; say we must pay 'tax' to keep our own business."

"You pay?"

She scoffs. "Me? Pay? No way, man. I tell them to kiss my black ass. Next thing I know, my cousin gets shot outside his own bar, and I got two choices: stay and end up next or leave and start new life somewhere they don't know my name."

I stare at her, suddenly understanding something behind her

sharp tongue and big laughs. "So, you came to London."

"London, Paris, Madrid, back to London. Trying to keep low, trying to stay out of trouble." She laughs, but it is bitter as bad kumis. "And look where I end up—sitting with you, in fake Kazakh restaurant, after being nearly strangled by taxi meter prices. Trouble always find me."

I sip my drink, nodding slow. "Is same for me. In my country, trouble find you even when you hide in mountains."

Mfanni grins. "Then maybe is good we find each other, yeah? You got your Kazakh hustle; I got my Jamaican hustle. Two hustlers together."

I clink glass against hers. "Two hustlers together. Just don't try charge me 'tax' on my beshbarmak."

She bursts into laughter so loud even fake-Kazakh Arsen peeks over from kitchen.

Then bill come: 169 pounds! Fake-Arsen stand there looking proud like rooster who think he own whole farm. I pretend English money still new to me (thank you, acting classes from Zhanakorgan Community Center).

"My friend," I say to Mfanni loud enough for whole restaurant to hear, "this man think we made of gold? In my country, this much money feed whole village for week!"

Fake-Arsen face turn red as communist flag. "No, no! Is normal price for horse meat!"

"Normal price? You think we stupid?" I gasp like shocked like babushka finding vodka in priest's pocket. "Back home, meat cost nothing - we have more horses than people! But here you charge fortune for portion size of mouse ear? No! Never!"

He start shouting at Mfanni about payment, which big mistake. Nobody yell at my new friend who has octopus-kiss powers.

"Listen, my arse Vlad," I say (mixing English words make insult more powerful). "You want piece of meat? I show you piece of meat – when I cut off yours!"

Then magic happen! He throw us out, saying never come back. In Zhanakorgan, we call this "winning by losing." But best part? Mfanni grab him in bear hug, push his rat face into her magnificent chest. His angry Russian screams turn into sweet music, muffled by what we call in my country "natural sound dampeners."

First time all night he sound like real Kazakh! Maybe there hope for him after all. But probably not.

London teaching me many things: sometimes best dinner is free dinner, best revenge is creative revenge, and best friends are ones who know how to use their assets in emergency situations.

I think I going to like this city very much.

CHAPTER 4

The Zig-Zag Club

S o now me and Mfanni, full of Zhaya and victory, decide we need proper drinks. Flying Tyshkan not serve alcohol because "no license" (I think real reason is they afraid what happen when real Kazakh meet fake Kazakh after vodka).

"What kind drink you want?" I ask Mfanni. She say whiskey, which make my heart sing like drunk shepherd. We already sisters from different continents! She tell me she know special club with free whiskey. My new friend getting more interesting than Zhanakorgan soap opera.

"You my London teacher!" I say excited. She make face like she bite lemon when I say "hostess" though. Note to self: some English words more dangerous than unexploded bomb.

We catch taxi, and this time I not even need threaten driver with ancient Kazakh curse. Mfanni just say "Zig-Zag Club", and taxi man drive straight there. At end, driver not even want payment! Very strange - in Zhanakorgan, only time taxi free is when driver is your cousin (and even then, he probably steal your wallet).

Club is in basement, dark. I can only see Mfanni's teeth and eyes floating in darkness, like Cheshire Cat from Alice story (thank you, English teacher, for cultural education). Big men at door let us in free, smiling as if they know secret I don't know. Starting to think maybe my friend Mfanni have special powers, like wizard from Harry Potter books (also thank you, English teacher).

Then this big man appear from darkness, talking funny English: "Hey mah lickle chickadees." (I think maybe he need English teacher too). He do weird eye thing at me - wank? wink? English language very confusing about eye movements. Mfanni seem know him but not happy way, like when you see relative who always want borrow money.

We get whiskey at bar - also free! In Zhanakorgan we have saying: "When fox offer free chicken, check if you still have both kidneys."

Then I see small man behind us, wearing suit sharp enough to cut bread. He paying for drinks, have strange little mustache. Tiny man, bald as peeled onion, mustache twitching like nervous caterpillar. He leans against bar, eyes jumping from girl to girl. His hand disappears into pocket, then comes out, then disappears again – maybe it has own secret agenda.

I feel his gaze land on me, and my back suddenly itch like mosquito bite. "New face?" he says, voice greasy as leftover kebab paper.

I pretend not hear.

"New talent," he repeats, stepping closer, his breath a mix of whiskey and something that might be sweat or desperation.

"What kind of talent?" I ask, because curiosity is my worst problem in life.

He smiles, showing teeth too perfect to belong to honest man. London talent," he says. "Special talent."

"Thank you for drinks," I say to him. "What's in it for us?" Mfanni look at me like I just suggest we milk male horse.

"Ha ha, I'm Bernard," he say, trying to be smooth. I tell him my name Lapshagul, introduce Mfanni. Then he make big mistake - call me "Lap Dance Girl" and make joke about Mfanni's name that make me want introduce him to traditional Kazakh wrestling moves.

"Hey, Small Mustache Man," I say (using polite version of what I thinking), "you trying be funny or you just stupid like yak with university degree?"

He back away little bit (smart move), start talking about buying presents and drinks. Mfanni suddenly become businesswoman, demand whiskey AND champagne. Then she say thing that make my ears blush: "If you soften us up, maybe we make you go hard."

I look at Mfanni with new eyes. In Zhanakorgan, we have saying: "Never judge book by cover but maybe check if book actually snake in disguise." Starting to think my new friend have many chapters I not read yet.

This night turning interesting - beautiful to watch but maybe dangerous to join. But in London, seems everything free have price tag hiding in dark corner. Good thing I learn art of Kazakh self-defense (mostly involves shouting and creative threats about livestock).

CHAPTER 5

Bernard and the Pole Dance

After three bottles of fancy bubble drink, me and Mfanni sit with Small Mustache Bernard like bread in sandwich. Mfanni getting very friendly - her hand disappear under table. I sit far away because situation remind me of time my uncle's prize goat eat bad mushrooms - things about to get weird.

Then I see big man from before (who I now call Vertigo because he make my head spin with anger) giving Mfanni special look. She get up, walk to silver pole in middle of room that go from floor to ceiling like metal tree with no branches.

What happen next make my eyes want jump out of head and run back to Zhanakorgan! Mfanni start dancing with pole like it her long-lost lover.

This not beautiful dance such as great Aigul Kossanova with traditional dombra - this more what drunk Russian soldiers do when vodka kill last brain cell.

I run to save my friend (because in Zhanakorgan, we never leave sister behind, even if sister we just meet today). But when I try help, her top decide to become rebel - suddenly boom! One boob escape, I try help push it back to prison, but then all men start howling like wolves seeing full moon.

"More! More!" they shout, pack of hungry dogs wearing pants. Vertigo yell, "Nice stuff girls, keep going!" Now both Mfanni's assets doing freedom dance in air, and my skirt climbing up legs like it trying reach moon. If it go any higher, my private parts will become public entertainment!

"Mfanni!" I say in panic voice, "We must exit stage left immediately!" But she pull away, her angry face not matching dancing body, like puppet with wrong head. "Let me make my money," she screech, "or join me for good profit!"

So there we stand - me with skirt trying reach heaven, Mfanni's chest doing independent performance, while dirty old men throw money at us. Even get pink fifty-pound notes – at home only time I see pink money is when someone wash red sock with white bills.

All the drinking and dancing make me need to piss. Outside of toilet, hear voice from man room. It is Bernard! He speaking perfect Kazakh into phone: "Yes, target acquired. She's exactly as described. Will proceed as planned." My heart doing gymnastics in chest, but when I get back to table, there he is just simple Bernard again, smiling like baby who needs diaper change.

Behind me, Mfanni is finally done. She wobbles back to the table, makeup slightly smeared, but holding up two crisp fifty-pound notes like she just won Olympic gold.

"That," she gasps, dropping onto her seat, "was easiest money I ever made."

I stare at her, then at Bernard, who just reappeared . "That was something," I mutter.

Then Vertigo comes over to the table, starts talking about "percentages" like we running small business instead of big embarrassment.

His words work like cold shower on Mfanni. She knows this game—first they talk about "percentages," then suddenly you're not the one making decisions anymore.

We fix clothes quicker than horse after bee sting, rush past

Vertigo, upstairs, into fresh London air. Men cheer as if we famous performers. Ha! In Zhanakorgan, this kind fame make grandmother die from shame twice.

Outside, breathing hard, I ask Mfanni why she do pole dance. But answer clear as tank tracks in snow - she know this business, probably work here before. This jezökşe business - yes, we have in my country too, but I come to London for different dream. Want maybe open restaurant, or make traditional dombra for fancy Harrods store, not dance with metal stick while old men throw money.

We exchange phone numbers like proper London ladies, pretending nothing strange happen. "Must go home," she say. "Yes, me too," I reply, thinking maybe some paths better not walked, even if paved with pink fifty-pound notes.

Will I call her? Maybe. But wise woman in Zhanakorgan say (okay, maybe I make this up now): "When friend show you pole dance club, maybe time to find new friend who like regular coffee shop instead."

CHAPTER 6

The Fifty Pound Note

L et me tell you about morning after crazy night, when I wake up in my tiny room that make shoebox look like palace. In Zhanakorgan, we say size not matter, but clearly landlord in London never hear this saying.

I wake up feeling like entire circus performing inside my head – you know when whole herd of elephants decide to do dancing competition in your brain? Yes, that feeling. My head making dauylpaz noise (this special Kazakh drum – see? I teaching you culture while telling story about my shame. You welcome!).

But this not most interesting part. No, most interesting part is what I find when I scratch itchy place that polite people never mention in good company. There, hiding is surprise present nobody ask for, fifty-pound note from pervert man in basement club! Money so clean and crisp, with picture of Queen Elizabeth looking at me like she know exactly where this note been hiding. I think maybe she not so amused.

Queen look very fancy on money. Very proper. I look at her face and think maybe one day I also be queen – not of England, they already have too many, but queen of this crazy town. But then I think: is this how future queen should behave? Running around dark basements with Mfanni, doing strange things with strange men who have more money than sense? In home country, we have saying: "When sheep try to live like wolf, sheep end up as dinner anyway."

I look at myself in mirror of tiny room. No curtains on window because apparently in London, curtains are luxury item like gold teeth or proper heating. I see my reflection and think I look strong as farm girl should be – thanks to Uncle's farm where I learn lifting heavy things more useful than lifting fancy teacups. Uncle always say "Strong body make strong future" (he also say "Don't talk to strangers in dark clubs" but I ignore that advice).

But then I notice something else – across roof, through other window, is little man watching. Something about this man tickle my brain like forgotten word on tip of tongue. He wearing something weird – not normal person clothes. In Zhanakorgan, we say man who dress strange either artist or needs doctor, sometimes both. But something about him make me think maybe he exactly kind of man I should meet – quiet, lonely type who probably have more money than friends.

I get back in bed and think about future. Maybe this fifty-pound note teaching me lesson. Village wisdom says: "Smart bird not only knows how to fly – smart bird knows where to land." Maybe I need be smart bird in London, but first must figure out which trees have best branches, yes?

But most important question still giving me headache worse than mixing drinks: why little man across roof wearing what look like costume from ballet? This mystery for another time, after I find proper curtains. In London, seems everyone want free show, but smart Kazakh girl know – best performances always need ticket!

CHAPTER 7

Brady

Morning sun shine through window like golden spotlight from heaven, making me think of home. If you ask what color is Zhanakorgan, I tell you golden-yellow - color of warm hugs, family love, mother's cooking.

Why I leave this golden paradise? If you ask me now as I lay here, lazy in tiny London bed, maybe I pretend not know, but truth is as bottle of Stoli. Had to escape Zhanakorgan, where girls become old women at sixteen. I live like grandmother for sixteen more years, making me thirty- two - ancient in Tomenaryk village. But here in London? Thirty-two is spring chicken! Magic trick - move to London, become young again!

But London never be true home. Even if they give me British passport with fancy stamp, my blood still flow with rhythm of steppe, heart still beat to drums of ancestors. One day I return home - must return - but with achievements that make family proud. Not just stories about pole- dancing adventures and pink money.

These thoughts give me goosebumps (English word I learn - mean skin get bumpy like plucked chicken). Time to find shower, wash away memories of last night.

Go downstairs looking for Landlordlady, forgetting small detail that I wear birthday suit (in my country, we not so shy about bodies - big mistake in London, I learn very quick). Knock on ground floor door and old man open - his eyes get big like someone stuff whole roasted sheep in each socket. First time seeing naked Kazakh woman, I think. Poor man. "Sorry, where is shower?" I ask politely.

Suddenly Landlordlady appear, screaming words that would make sailor in Caspian Sea blush. "Get some clothes on, you dirty cow! You'll give Brady heart attack!"

Brady (must be old man with sheep eyes) now holding chest like he trying keep heart from jumping out. Face turn deep purple of Tomenaryk sunset. I run upstairs, hear ambulance coming with loud cry.

Peek downstairs, see them take Brady away with blanket over face. Oh, great spirits of steppe! I kill English man with naked body! Sit on bed shivering - sun now hide behind cloud like shy bride.

Landlordlady come up, try comfort me. Say Brady have bad heart anyway, death will be "accident." But in my country, if you kill someone with naked body, must give family many horses as compensation. Very worried about police.

Then strange thing happen. Landlordlady hug me - not normal hug but squeeze like python trying to eat large rabbit. Her chocolate arms wrap around me, hands moving... how you say... fumbling everywhere same as drunk man searching for keys in dark.

Now I have dilemma. Back home, we have two solutions for unwanted touching: 1) Scream like angry eagle, or 2) Use ancient art of Qazaq Kuresi wrestling. Choose option two - more elegant, chess move but with body.

Quick as snake, I put arm around her neck, other arm behind knee, then-

BOOM!

She fly through air same as fat pigeon, make sound like balloon losing air. Land on bed, eyes close, white foam of rabid camel coming from mouth.

"Wake up!" I shout, slap face gentle (okay, maybe not so gentle), pinch nipple. She wake up, very angry, start screaming about police and molestation. Excuse me? Who molest who?

Then – knock-knock! Someone at door. Landlordlady run downstairs faster than I think possible for woman her size, screaming all way: "Just you wait, you perverted bitch!"

Hear her tell someone downstairs: "Come in, yes, she did it, she's upstairs."

In Zhanakorgan, we have saying (this one real, I swear): "When naked body cause two medical emergencies before breakfast, maybe time to buy bathrobe."

CHAPTER 8

Constable Clitter

L ooking downstairs, I see police helmet coming up slow like moon rising over steppe. Helmet have metal pimple silver thing on top. Man under helmet move careful, hunter stalking prey, while Landlordlady follow behind, mouth running more than river during spring flood.

"She killed Brady! Try to kill me too! Put her in handcuffs, Constable Clitter!" Landlordlady squawks.

Wait...Constable WHAT? In Kazakhstan, we have many strange names, but Clitter? I wonder if his first name Dick - would be too perfect, bad joke from comedy show.

Then he reach top of stairs, standing in front of me, great big sweating mountain in blue uniform. Buttons on chest shine like stars, breathing so heavy I worry maybe he join Brady in ambulance soon. I stand there shaking - from fear or from being naked as newborn foal, not sure.

Landlordlady still making broken radio noise behind him: "Arrest this slut! Lock her up! She doesn't belong in this country, she's a..."

"Oh, shut the fuck up!" say policeman, voice tired same as village elder who listen to thousand complaining grandmothers in one day. Then he look at me: "Go in your room and sit down."

I obey. He follows me in, close door in Landlordlady's face (ha!).

Then me and Constable Clitter have five-minute conversation that change my whole life like magic spell. Cannot tell details (some things better stay private, yes?), but when he finish "talking", he very relaxed. Walk out my room, go downstairs to speak with Landlordlady.

From upstairs, I hear only little bits: Landlordlady now sweet as honey, "Yes officer, no officer, of course officer." Different person! Then front door close, and I sit on bed thinking about what just happen in this crazy country called United Kingdom of Great Britain.

Feel bit strange - happy but also little bit disappointed, like when you expect big fight but get peaceful talk instead. And guess what? His name really is Dick! Dick Clitter - my new friend with power in London.

Sometimes life more funny than any joke.

After all excitement, I go downstairs again (still naked - why bother with clothes now?), find bathroom, take shower. Nobody dare say word to me. Put on proper clothes - jeans, t-shirt, trainers - and walk out into London streets feeling strong like warrior queen.

In Zhanakorgan, we have saying (this one I definitely make up right now): "When police officer named Dick Clitter save you from trouble, maybe universe trying tell you funny joke."

CHAPTER 9

Mfanni's Plan

L et me tell you about day when my friend Mfanni decide to show me new "career path" in London. (In my country, career path usually involve either herding sheep or government job. Here? Different kind of animals altogether.)

I feel good after morning adventure with Constable Funny Name, so when Mfanni call to meet, I say yes. She give me address in place called Cock Fosters (I already have enough trouble with one cock this morning- English language make everything sound dirty!)

Find Mfanni standing outside place called "Bare Essentials." In my country, bare essential mean bread and vodka. In London? Turn out it mean something very different.

Inside, place look fancy - not dark basement club style. Nice lady give us fluffy towels like we going to beach party. But surprise! No beach here - just lots of naked people walking around, maybe they forget where they put clothes! Me and Mfanni join naked parade (second time today for me - maybe this my new London hobby?).

Men look at us like hungry dogs look at meat truck. We get in hot tub with bubbles, and... how you say... interesting things start happening. Men keep joining, pretending they not looking but eyes almost fall out of heads. I worry what happening under water – back home, we have saying: "What float in public bath usually not rubber duck."

I want leave, but Mfanni say no - she see "opportunity." (In

Kazakhstan, when friend say "opportunity," usually mean either marriage proposal or pyramid scheme. Here? Who knows!)

Then biggest surprise come - like plot twist in bad movie. Who appear from back room? Vertigo! Same pimp from Zig-Zag club! He call us "blackie and whitey, fatty and skinny" as if we are circus act. I about to tell him where he can put his circus, but Mfanni grab my arm.

"Wait," she whisper. "This fit plan." (In Zhanakorgan, when plan involve man who call you names, plan usually end with someone losing teeth. But London different game with different rules.)

Next thing I know, they give us separate massage rooms. I look at setup: table with hole in end (why?), oil bottle, tissues... Kazakh massage mean someone walk on your back until spine make funny noise. Here? Different kind of noise expected, I think.

I go check on Mfanni (big mistake) and find her with customer called Henry. Poor Henry look like mouse caught between two cats - scared but maybe enjoying fear too much? When Mfanni tell me drop towel, I give quick show of natural Kazakh beauty then exit quicker than politician leaving scandal.

Get dressed and leave, watching Henry sneak out holding towel - precious state secrets in his hands, while next customer already lined up like hungry cat waiting outside fish market.

I learning many things about London business:

1. Everything have double meaning
2. Nothing free
3. Some "opportunities" cost more than money

In my country, we have saying: "When wolf dress as sheep, check if he selling wool." Today I think maybe London full of wolves selling different kinds of wool.

Time to think hard about what kind of London story I want

write for myself. Maybe one with more clothes and less..... "opportunity."

CHAPTER 10

Recruitment

L et me tell you story about how girl get pulled into London underground like potato into soup pot. After escape from naked spa in Cock Fosters (English people really need committee for better naming), I realize life pushing me down path I not expect.

Truth is, I come to London with simple dreams: maybe nice café where I serve shirchay, or shop selling fashions that not show all private parts.

But problem is, no money, no paper saying I smart (except one saying I graduate from School of Hard Knocks in Zhanakorgan, but London people not impressed by this).

Plan was find rich husband on internet - you know, Tindy, Grindy, all these apps where people pretend they better looking than real life. But my friend Mfanni? She believe in more... direct approach. Like bulldozer direct.

Back at my tiny room in Shepherds Bush (another name that make no sense - see no shepherds, only pigeons), find surprise guest: Constable Dick Clitter sitting on my bed as if he own place. He holding his helmet (real one for head, not... other kind - after morning's adventure, must be specific about these things).

Landlordlady look at floor when I come in - defeated bear wrestler after bad match. Ha! Now she know this girl not so easy to push around!

I make tea for police man because in my country, even when someone try blackmail you in morning, you still show manners in afternoon. He take tea with two sugar, much milk - sweet like his corrupt little heart.

Then come proposal. Not marriage kind (thank Allah), but maybe worse. He say "I think you got something I want." I laugh because... well, he already see everything this morning when I naked and need help with dead Brady situation. But no - he have different idea.

Turn out London police work like Kazakh police - they also use people for spying! But difference is they usually make family spy on family.

Here? They want me spy on Vertigo, pimp man who run both Zig-Zag club and naked spa. Small world in London underground - like village, but with more criminals wearing fancy suits.

When Clitter say "we" instead of "I", I know game changing. Back home, when one person become "we," usually mean either marriage proposal or KGB getting interested. Here? Mean police want piece of action too.

He hands me two twenty-pound notes (because even fighting crime need proper payment in London). Then this fool try kiss me with his big blue lips! I tell him kiss only allowed on face cheeks, not... other cheeks. Must be very specific with English people - they worse than lawyer for finding loopholes!

Then he grabs back one of the twenties! Say it was "fine" for trying bribe him with naked body this morning. He claim his... special police equipment... fall out by accident when getting wallet. Ha! In Zhanakorgan, we have saying: "When wolf say he vegetarian, count your sheep twice."

Before leaving, he promise make me rich as informant. I think maybe this better than Mfanni's plan of showing special Kazakh beauty to sad men in spa. At least with police work, can keep clothes on. Usually.

Now I have new job: spy on bad guys for maybe-also-bad guys in uniform. Is like those Russian matryoshka dolls that fit inside each other - open one bad guy, find another inside!

Look out window at mysterious bald man in building across way. He writing something, maybe also report about crazy immigrant girl who keep getting into trouble? Who know - in London, seems everybody either criminal or spy. Sometimes both!

In my country, we say when dance with devil, make sure you wear fireproof underwear. In London? Better wear waterproof everything - too many people spitting in soup!

CHAPTER 11

Abdul Ameer

My head spins like carousel in village fair - too many things happening in London life! Money situation not good, but I refuse to use brother's magic money card. No, no - Lapshagul must prove she is strong independent woman. Maybe walk will help clear fuzzy brain.

So, I leave fancy Bush area, through place called Hammersmith (why they name place after tool? English people very strange), down to big river Thames. Almost call Mfanni, but she is like sugar cube in tea - sweet but dissolves your good sense very quick. Think about PC Clitter instead - still waiting for him to give spy instructions about catching mysterious Vertigo man. Money not much for such dangerous game, but pfft! I am Kazakh woman - we wrestle bears for fun in my village.

Walking by river, boats going toot-toot on left side, bicycle people going ding-ding on right side. Sun doing what English sun does best - hiding behind cloud, peeking out, hiding again. But still, is beautiful day. At least things happening to me now - not good things maybe, but better than village life where most exciting event was when neighbor's cow eat grandmother's best dress. Here, I feel alive! Like bird who escape cage, even if bird sometimes crash into window.

Think about my brother, how he make Kazakhstan look silly but become very rich. But I make different promise to self: Borat make joke of country, but Lapshagul will be elegant as swan! (Even if swan sometimes step in dog poo on London street).

I giggling at this thought when voice behind me ask, "What's funny?" Turn around to see man in Muslim clothes with beard that look like it forget to grow in middle. Oh blyad, I think, not another religious lecture I get back home!

"What you want? Go away! Had enough lectures about proper behavior back in village!" I tell him.

But he surprise me: "Don't be like that! I'm Abdul Ameer - London's most intoxicated Muslim!"

Ha! Now this interesting! Back home, saying goes: "Strange bird make interesting song." Maybe this strange bird worth listening to?

"Okay, Abdul," I say, trying to sound like street-smart London girl, "you buy drink then?"

"What's your poison, sister?" he ask.

"Whiskey," I say, thinking how grandmother would faint if she hear me now. "Strong like horse kick."

He say follow him for good time, and I thinking: what crazy soup am I jumping into now? But English have saying - beggars cannot be choosers. (Though why beggar would want to choose anything except money is mystery to me).

One hour later, we drinking and laughing, and not once does he mention Allah or show me proper way to pray. Very suspicious. Why he dress as holy man but act like party animal? When I ask, he lean close, breath stinking with fumes of his bad choices, and whisper secret that make my eyebrows jump to hairline...

Abdul whispers secret to me: "I dress this way so authority leaves me alone. I can do whatever I want - take from shops, cause trouble - police too scared to stop me because they fear being called Islamophobic!"

I think this story sounds as believable as cow giving cola, but then he takes me to Boots the Chemist. Before I can blink twice, he's stuffing things under his clothes like squirrel hiding nuts for winter! Security watching but doing nothing! Then - disaster! He hands me box, says "Hide this," and vanishes.

Big security man stops me. "Are you with him?" he asks, face like angry potato. I try innocent face - one that worked on Papa when breaking his tractor. "With who?" Wrong move! They drag me to back room, find box under my shirt. Durex condoms! Ya Allah, if Mama could see me now!

"We can't touch him because he's Muslim, but you're going to jail!" security man says, proud like rooster who just win medal in chicken beauty contest.

"But I'm Muslim too!" I try. Fat shop lady laughs. "You? In that mini skirt? Real Muslim girl wouldn't steal condoms - you probably working girl!"

This is outrage! I am Kazakh princess, not some... Then who walks in but PC Dick Clitter! My relief lasts shorter than snowman in desert. "Oh my God! Dickie Clit!" I say with joy.

"Shut mouth!" he shouts. "Call me that again, I'll kick your ass until it's black and yellow!"

Must admit - his insults improving! I give him biggest smile. "Sorry, officer! You rescue me from these fascists who plant naughty items on innocent girl while letting terrorist Abdul the Bulbul Ameer escape?"

He doesn't answer, just drags me to police station, throws me in cell that's hot like sauna, no water except in toilet - and I may be from backward country, but not that desperate! After removing layers until just underwear remains, I lay on plastic mattress that's stickier than honey.

Two hours later, PC Clitter appears. Says he paid for condoms; charges dropped. I laugh, asking what police officer needs with so many condoms - maybe for making balloon animals?

"They're for you," he says. "You'll use them how I say." "Forget it, Clit! Not doing anything with rubber balloons!"

"You will, or I tell shop to press charges. Then you go prison with three very friendly lady cellmates!"

So here I am, thinking day cannot get worse. Started with crazy policeman wanting me to be spy, now he threatens me with prison full of angry women if I don't do something with box of protection! And it's only afternoon - in home, bad luck waits until evening at least! This PC Clitter thinks he can push around vulnerable Kazakh princess? Time to show him what happens when you mess with girl who wrestled wolves for fun!

"Fine, Officer," I say sweetly. He screams, "That's Constable Clitter to you!"

Wow, someone needs to calm down about their silly name. Not my fault his parents hate him.

"Sorry," I say, "Can I call you Dick?"

"No, you bloody can't! It's Officer or Mr. Clitter!" he shouts, face turning color of beetroot soup.

CHAPTER 12

Dancing with Devils

So, Vertigo, condoms, queen of the town, and so and etcetera - aren't I a busy Kazakh princess, eh? Yes, a very busy Kazakh princess, but so far, I've only been surviving, defending myself, like cage fighter with back to fence. I'm now thinking I should get off fence and take fight forward - after all, I am my brother's sister!

Back in my room, I get prepared to take on world as superwoman who I really am. I change clothes to tight and slinky outfit, with high black boots, high neck collar, and long cuffs. I put big rings on fingers and tie hair back, very tight and very high. My makeup is white with black eyes and last item is motorcycle jacket with many silver studs.

I go downstairs and look in the full-length mirror in the hallway. I am pleased by what I see. Landlordlady comes out of her kitchen, takes one look at me, and screams, "Argh! Lapshagul, you are terrifying!"

I grin, baring my teeth. "Good," I tell her. "And you'd better keep my rent low, or I'll be even more terrifying!"

She narrows her eyes, shaking her head like she's seen something she doesn't quite understand. Then, in a quieter voice, she mutters, "You got something, girl. People do what you say, even when they don't want to. That ain't normal." Her eyes linger on me a beat longer. "That's power."

It is getting late, and sun is going down. I decide to call Mfanni, she agrees to meet me outside Zig-Zag club. I take cab and when

I arrive, I grumble and complain but pay driver with much dramatic sighing. Is highway robbery, these London prices! In Kazakhstan, this money would buy whole herd of finest goats!

I see Mfanni at door of club, she has been watching my theatrical payment performance. "That was brilliant," she says, with her big, beautiful smile. I walk towards her, and she looks me up and down. "Fuck me!" she says, "you look great."

I thank her for compliment but decline offer to fuck her. I'm not a - how you say - a muff-diver, or clam-gobbler, or gender no-hole, or even bi-cyclical. I am Kazakh princess and I'm going to be famous as superwoman.

We go into club and walk down dark stairs. It is quiet, not many people have arrived yet. But Vertigo is standing at bar wearing white suit, and his hair is now dyed white. I say, "Hey, Vertigo, you look like fucking negative film!" He had grinned at me, but his grin turns into fierce snarl, he says, "You racist bitch! Look at yourself, coming in here dressed like that! What are you trying to prove to me?"

I answer him loudly, "I'm not trying to prove anything to you, you money- grabbing pimp, I don't need you, I can look after myself, you are just blood-sucking suluk!" Then he gives me big surprise because his snarl turns into massive grin and he starts to laugh, starting with deep voice then going up octaves to high pitch. "Heh, heh, heeeh! I'm likin' your spirit mah girl, innit, hey, I'm liking your spirit, so I'ze wanting to see for myself what you can do to make us both big money."

Wow, I'm thinking that I'm getting close here, getting close to being very good and powerful undercover spy for Police Constable Detective Dickus Clitterus, or whatever his name is that I keep forgetting. I'm thinking that I've got Vertigo on end of my fishing hook, and I'm wrapping him around my little nipple... or is it little finger, I need to learn your expressions better.

"And how do you want to see for yourself Vertigo?" I ask him, with my eyebrows up and my head on tilt to one side. And also fold my arms across chest for added effect of keeping power and distance. Another trick I use is to stare down at place between his legs where there is bulge and imagine that bulge is made by swollen fat pussy, instead of donga, and this makes me giggle.

Vertigo gets angry again and his grin disappears, "What are you fuckin' sniggering at, you fucking Kazakh whore? Stop looking at my manhood!"

I reply, "Are sure it is manhood in there? And not a pizda?"

"What's a fuckin' pizda, you gobby little moppet?!" he shouts. I reply that pizda is what woman does piss from. That does it, "Right, get in here, now!" And then he grabs and pulls me into back room. Mfanni is already in this room, and she closes door behind me.

"Mfanni!" I say, "Are you on his side? Are you helping him, you are against me!" She looks like she is proud to be Vertigo's gangsta-moll.

Vertigo bare his teeth in what supposed to be smile. "Welcome to team, Lapshaggy! You'll be proper money-maker for us, yeah? Like striking oil in bloody Hackney - and we're gonna milk this cash cow till she runs dry!"

Now, I'm thinking that it is totally and super important that Mfanni doesn't know about my problem that I must come up with clever solution for. It's true that me and her have our own plan together, but she must never not ever know about my lying-under motivations. In other words, if she find out about me and Dick Clitter I think I'll be very dead London Kazakh princess! My mind has no doubts that Mfanni and Vertigo are maybe having sexy times with each other, going at it same as two marmots fighting over last piece of grass before winter - though in my country, this very normal. Here in London, people probably think marmot is type of fancy French cheese.

These are my thinkings as me and Mfanni get out of cab and go into Bare Essentials Naturist Relaxation Lounge in Foster's Cock. "Hey, my chickadees!" says Vertigo. He kisses Mfanni but doesn't kiss me - he hasn't yet forgiven me for previous unfortunate incident. I'm not blaming him, I suppose, but I kind of want to apologise. I start to say sorry but he interrupts me, 'No, don't apologise, you're dirty fucker and I hate you, but dirty fuckers make money and I've got work for you.'

Mfanni says, "Yes, that's good, and I'll look after her, let us work together! We can be Dynamic Duo, Syncro Sisters...Four Hands Firm!" And suddenly Mfanni is successfully selling our idea to Vertigo. Off he goes into reception area of Foster's Cock establishment, leaves me and Mfanni together in this little room with massage table in it.

I say to my friend, "Hey, remember what we agreed – you do all stuff, I'm not doing any touching of todgers or goolies, cocks or balls, pendys or nyktars, whatever you want to call pervy men's sexing equipment, I don't touch, okay Mfanni, got that?" She is nodding hard and saying,"Yes, yes, I agree, don't worry, Shaggy, I know the terms of our deal." Hmmm, I think, yes, you know terms of our deal, but you don't know terms of deal between me and detective Dick the Clit.

So, I'm pleased with way this is going, feeling like I have situation under control. Then there's knock on door and Juicy Lucy comes in. "Hi guys," she says, "We've got customer for you, insisting on half hour with you both, except that he doesn't want four hands, he wants two hands and two feet."

We are surprised by weird and deviant request, but I quite like idea of using my feet, it seems kind of acceptable. I say, "Okay, Juice babe, show him in!"

Mfanni is kind of doubtful about this, I don't think she understands, or I don't think she wants to walk on man in case she squashes him with her big yurt-sized chocolate body. I tell her not to worry, I will do foot stuff as I am very good Cossack dancer.

Then Juicy shows this short fat man called Roger into our room and Mfanni tells him to take off his clothes. He does this and I pretend to be all embarrassed and shy, which is plan that me and Mfanni will use to get customers all excited and then maybe they give bigger tips and come back for more massages in future.

"Oooh, tee, hee," I say with squeaky voice, "Please cover yourself up, I am highly qualified Muslim masseuse, and I am forbidden from looking at cocks!" Short fat customer laughs at me and looks at Mfanni. She says to him, "Don't take any notice of her, she's new here, she'll get used to it, and she'll be one to be using her feet."

Roger lies down on table on his front and I take off my shoes and trousers stand up on table just in my top and knickers and start using my feet on his hairy spotty back and treading on him. Mfanni uses her hands all over his body and between cheeks either side of anoos. He starts to moan, and I put more weight on him with my feet, and he is grunting like pig, "Oink, oink, oink!"

"Louder, little piggy, squeal louder so we can hear you!" All time I'm really walking hard on his squishy hairy back. Mfanni pours baby oil on him, and I slip sometimes, and I nearly fall off, but I manage to keep my balance and I think of my first attempts at skating on frozen lake near my village.

Grunting and squealing gets louder and louder and I'm trying not to look but I can see that Mfanni has her hand between piggy Roger's bumcheeks, and I think that she is probably tickling his plums because suddenly he lets out this final moan, he seems to puff up and then shrivel with farty noise.

I think it's time to get off him, so I jump down onto floor. Mfanni is wiping her hands with Kleenex tissue. "There you are Roger," she says to customer, "your balls are nice and empty now, so you can go home relax, but first you must give us some of your lovely money."

Roger gets dressed slowly with guilty expression on face, he takes out his wallet and gives two hundred pounds to Mfanni, he then walks out and Mfanni gives £100 to me. All done in less than quarter of one hour. Nice work, I'm thinking, and I didn't do even one bit of rudeness.

Then we go out of room and into reception area of establishment and Vertigo is there and he's very pleased, "Well done, my chickadees, that guy just booked you again for next week and you have two more in waiting room now! We're gonna call your service 'Walkabout Willie Massage', it'll get massive following."

At night's end, me and Mfanni leave Bare Essentials with five hundred sterling pounds each. Mfanni whines about her sore wrist, and I pretend not to hear her playing imaginary dombra - such musical talent, this one!

It's ten o'clock, and because we are now rich London ladies (ha!), we decide to celebrate our new business arrangement.

"I know good place!" says Mfanni. Of course you do, I think. Mfanni knows everything about London, like personal walking Google Maps with extra sass. "Okay," I say, "let's go have good time." I'm thinking, hey, life not so bad! I have many Sterling pounds, good face, good body, and in U and K, I'm still young woman! Not in my country, where at 32, I'm practically babushka, spending days worrying about everything from morning till night.

I follow Mfanni upstairs (funny, usually we go downstairs in these places) to club where we must pay to enter and get bags searched. We both have protection in bags, but security people don't care - they want weapons, maybe drugs. Though they search so badly, maybe just weapons. This place called Bedlam club and bozhe moy! It's crazy house! Music so loud my ears want to run away, lights flash so much, I think maybe I am having religious experience.

Mfanni starts dancing same as barefoot man who step on electric fence. I try to copy her, but my body only knows Kazakh moves. So, what do I do? I start doing Kara-Zhorga dance, full village style! Everyone crowds around like I am performing magic trick. Mfanni screams, "Go for it, Shaggy!" Soon, whole club trying to dance like drunk Kazakh at wedding. Very cultural exchange, yes? Then music changes, I collapse in chair, and nice men (not perverts, surprise!) buy us drinks.

I see Mfanni slip money to man in corner. Maybe he is drink waiter, I think, but ha! I may be from village, but I wasn't born yesterday in yurt. Still, tonight I decide not to care. Drinks keep coming, more dancing, and I learn to move like Mfanni - sexy city girl, not village idiot. Club closes four A.M., we stumble to street, my head floating off my shoulders.

Then - surprise! - I see little bald man who lives behind my flat. My eyes bit fuzzy from drinks, so there are two of him, but even with double vision, I know this man. What he doing here? In crazy London club? Must be Kazakh spy - why else would man with head like peeled egg be in such place?

When club closes, Mfanni hugs goodbye and goes off with "definitely- not-waiter" man. I decide to walk home because fresh air good for head that feels like someone stuff it with drunk butterflies doing belly dance. But something strange happening - whole world start to spin, and I keep thinking I'm back in Zhanakorgan with children throwing flowers at me.

Then nearly get hit by black taxi because I forget London cars don't stop for dreaming Kazakhs.

Back in my Bush house, in tiny room, I check window - no light in baldy spy's room. Lay on bed, fully dressed, watching ceiling do circus tricks. Thinking about spy man - how he find me? Must be Kazakh Friendship Centre - some friendship! Helping secret police instead of poor me!

Don't know if sleeping or awake, but mind happy now. Have money for Landlordlady, maybe buy fancy Gucci things from Harrods. Should take dance classes too, maybe get lips done like English girls. Mfanni lucky - has natural big lips. Mine are pencil lines, need pump up for London style.

Now definitely dreaming - see happy little boy, playing with toy truck on wooden floor in village near Zhanakorgan. Yellow light warm like summer sun, child's eyes green as spring grass, smile white like steppe snow. Yes, now I sleep, dream of home, while London darkness watches through window.

CHAPTER 13

The Business Plan

Beautiful London morning - feel powerful, like eagle soaring over steppe! Take cold bath (still not understanding why English houses have hot water if everyone take cold shower), then march self to Knightsbridge Street with money burning hole in pocket.

Treat self as proper Kazakh president's third wife - which means spending money quicker than drunk oligarch in casino. Soon have only ten Sterling left, not even enough for Landlordlady's rent. But new clothes make me proper rich bitch - someone who eat caviar for breakfast and wipe mouth with fifty-pound notes.

Call Constable Clitter, trying to be sweet as honey cake. "Officer, hello! How are you?" He growls back same as bear with hemorrhoid who mistake cactus for toilet paper: "What do you fucking want?"

"Need expense money for undercover work, please." Try to make voice smooth as spy in James Bond movie.

"Got any actual information, you useless..." Rest of words not suitable for polite company. Remind me about "trouble" he will bring if no results soon. Hang up phone feeling part kicked puppy; part hungry wolf ready to bite back.

Add his name to special Kekalu list - where I keep names of people who will one day have very bad accident involving angry goat and bottle of top shelf vodka.

Call Mfanni next - my favorite partner in crime, even though she probably lead me to trouble faster than drunken yak in China shop. Plan to meet at Zig Zag, then Bare Essentials for money making. She also spent all cash - probably on whatever not-waiter was selling in club.

At Zig Zag, Vertigo dressed like cotton candy exploded on him - bright pink suit, red shirt, looking like fairground snack. He say I look beautiful, which make me feel bad about candy comment. So, we work hard - me doing flirty smile routine while Mfanni do... whatever she doing under tables with Kleenex. I pretend not to notice.

After few customers, Mfanni complain: "Why you always do the flirting while I do the tugging? My arm is tired!" Tell her am allergic to man-juice - last time break out in rash worse than time tried to use week-old kumis as face cream. She look at me funny but accept excuse. Suggest we go to Bare Essentials - Vertigo taking too big slice of pie here anyway.

In cab to Foster's Cock, plan our famous Hands and Feet routine, dream big about own establishment – the McDonald's of massage parlors! First customer has surprise package - tall lady with massive chest mountains. But when Mfanni tell her turn over... surprise! Lady have extra equipment in underwear department. I almost fall through floor in shock. Mfanni shouts "Nice willie!" same as village elder admiring new racing horse.

Then customer try turning massage room into water park - we escape flying through air like Ninja warriors!

Charge extra for surprise show - five hundred pounds! Customer pay without complaint, probably used to premium rates for premium equipment. Two more normal customers (boring!), then pay room fee to Juicy Lucy.

Head to Bedlam club (guard own drink like mother hen – must have learned lesson about Mfanni's chemical experiments). See Vertigo appear, dancing with Mfanni. Think she playing dangerous game, but then I realize - London is all dangerous games. Without Mfanni's crazy schemes, would probably be selling sad kebabs to drunk English people who think spicy sauce is form of torture.

Mfanni come with news - Vertigo know about perfect place for our business. Near Hammersmith, he only want twenty percent! Think to self: do I really want work with man dressed as pimp from cartoon? But then remember - in London, must sometimes dance with devil to get ahead. If want be Princess, must let cash be King! Besides, location make me smile like cat who found cream - right next to the nick! Maybe Detective Clit-face can watch our little business meeting from his window while eating sad sandwich. Universe sometimes have excellent timing.

CHAPTER 14

Taban Bederi

So there's Vertigo, standing on corner like some fancy businessman from TV show, except normal businessmen don't usually have hair color of radioactive banana.

"Ay up, my little chickadees!" he shouts when he spots us, all teeth and yellow hair. "Punctual as Big Ben, innit!" I'm thinking to myself, yes, and you're about as subtle as nuclear explosion in tea party.

Mfanni does her sweet-girl routine, which makes Vertigo puff up like proud peacock. He leads us down alley that looks exactly like place where people in British crime shows find dead bodies. But surprise- surprise! Inside is actual proper room, with bonus bathroom that's smaller than my grandmother's pickle jar. Plus massage table that's seen better days, probably around time of Russian Revolution.

Vertigo says we use place for free, just tiny-weeny twenty percent cut for him. What generosity! Like wolf offering sheep discount on being eaten. Mfanni nods yes more than bobblehead in earthquake. Me, I just think, if things go bad, I run.

He fixes place up nice - new carpet that doesn't smell like feet, fresh paint that probably covers interesting stories, security camera outside that connects to phones (very James Bond, yes?). I suggest we put sign saying "Taban Bederi" - little joke about massage parlor, but Vertigo gets all huffy and calls me stupid Kazakh cow. I fire back with not-so-nice word, and holy borscht, everything explodes! Even Mfanni, who usually laughs at everything, gives me look that could freeze vodka. I say sorry because sometimes pride must bow to business, yes?

We celebrate at Flying Tishkan, because nothing says "new business partnership" better than meal at restaurant where health inspector afraid to eat. We tell Vertigo eating beshbarmak will make him hung like horse - old Kazakh saying I make from thin air.

Head waiter watching Vertigo way bomb squad eye suspicious package, so I do little side mission to kitchen. Few words here, few winks there, maybe small bribe (is called "cultural exchange" in diplomatic circles).

Result? They serve Vertigo plate with horse pizda, all dressed up pretty with herbs, ready for royal wedding! Instead of getting angry, he laughs so hard I think he might die, which would be inconvenient for business plan. He even pays bill, proving maybe even pimps have sense of humor hiding under all that fake designer clothing.

We all go separate ways, agreeing to meet tomorrow at what I still want to call Taban Bederi (is good joke if you know meaning!). Maybe Vertigo not completely terrible person. Like they say in old country - even snake has nice smile before it bites you. But maybe, just maybe, this snake only wants to do business.

CHAPTER 15

The Swing of Things

Mfanni waits for me next morning with news that makes me roll eyes so hard they almost see my brain - Vertigo is too busy making "interweb sight" at home. According to Mfanni, this magical thing will make phones go buzz-buzz with messages from desperate men wanting to throw money at us.

As if universe wants to prove point, my phone immediately makes rings. Message says "Hello darling, want to worship your precious toes!" I show Mfanni, who laughs like hyena who found particularly funny dead zebra. She tells me to send address of Taban Bederi, which I do, thinking London men are more strange than camels in snowstorm.

Vertigo gives Mfanni two keys - she hands me one like it's golden ticket to Willy Wonka's house of pervert chocolate. We wait inside like hunters, except instead of deer, we wait for sweaty men with too much money and too little shame.

After thirty minutes that feel longer than winter in steppes, doorbell rings. Who walks in? Fat hairy Roger from Bare Essentials – pudding face and pregnant yak belly. At least I know what comes next: me doing shy Muslim girl act (Allah forgive), him making noises like pig who found truffle in mud, disgusting things happening that would make my grandmother's spirit leave body twice, and Mfanni using entire forest worth of tissues. He leaves me two hundred pounds, richer in wallet, poorer in dignity.

Then comes Vertigo with camera, wanting to make "art" for

interweb. Mfanni gets excited like puppy seeing treat - "Oooh, yes Vertigo baby!" She does dance that would make belly dancers in Kazakhstan hang up their bells in shame. Meanwhile, I'm standing there thinking this is definitely not what mama meant when she said, "go make something of yourself in big city."

But before I can protest, door burst open and in walk three men walk in, moving through club like shadows with muscles. Leader stands in doorway, light catching metal pins in his jaw - souvenir from somebody's fist, I'm guessing. His friends loom behind him, matching tattoos crawling up necks like poisonous vines. Vertigo's whole mood changes when he sees them.

"Ballsak!" he calls out, voice dripping respect like honey from broken hive. "Welcome to my humble establishment!"

This Ballsak moves closer, each step calculated like chess player sizing up board. His eyes - one real, one glass - scan room as if taking inventory. When he speaks, his voice reminds me of rusty door hinge needing oil.

"These your new girls?" Ballsak asks Vertigo.

"Best in business," Vertigo says proud like father showing off prize cow. "Especially this one." He points at me. "Borat's sister!"

Mfanni whispers in my ear: "Albanian mafia. They own half of South London's worst secrets."

Vertigo leads them to dark corner where they speak in whispers sharp as razor blades. Me and Mfanni try to look busy, but ears working overtime like satellite dishes. After what feels like forever, Albanians melt away into night, leaving only chill in air and Vertigo's nervous smile.

Vertigo comes bouncing back to us, excited like child who just got new toy. Whatever deal they make must be good - he practically glowing with evil happiness.

"Your turn, Shaggy Tits!" Vertigo says to me; I give him look that could freeze Thames in summer.

"First, my tits not shaggy - they perfectly normal Kazakh tits. Second, your little camera not seeing my nunu today. I know these photos not for business - they for when you alone with hand and shame!"

"Oh, look who's too good for spreading legs! Princess Yurt thinks she's better than Mother Theresa now!"

Mfanni jokes, but jealousy smells stronger than yak butter in sun. Then she sees marks on my legs and bottom and then shuts up. We wait for next customer in silence that speaks louder than drunk English football fans.

I sit thinking about how life in London more complicated than advanced mathematics. In Zhanakorgan, things simple - you either have goat or you don't have goat. Here, everyone playing chess, but pieces keep changing shape. Maybe becoming Kazakh Superstar Princess in London take little more time than expected. But at least I learning - like father always say, "Smart fox learns new tricks, stupid fox ends up in pot."

I am putting on shoes again (so many shoes in one day!) when Mfanni does her welcome-welcome dance for new customer. She saying, "Come in, come in! But please to be gentle with my friend Lapshagul - she is fresh like morning bread and innocent as baby lamb!"

This man, he tells us he needs "therapeutic" massage (I learn quick in London - when they say therapeutic with little wink, is never about bad back).

"Must be very secret," he whispers. "Nobody can know I come here."

Then he sees me and his face does funny dance - ah! He expecting chocolate lady like Mfanni, but getting me instead. His eyes go big when he looks at me, and suddenly my brain does little jump - Bozhe moy! Is DJ from Bedlam club! Same one who plays boom-boom music that makes everyone wiggle bottoms like crazy people!

I tell him strip-strip and lie down, then grab Mfanni arm and pull her to corridor. "You know who this is?" I whisper-shout.

Mfanni's smile get so big, remind me of uncle Boltok after he win three sheep in poker game.

Then Mfanni - this crazy woman - pulls paper from her knickers (why she keeping papers there? Is not proper filing system).

"Look!" she says, "I write special song for customers. Maybe DJ man should hear first, yes?"

This idea seem brilliant, so we go back inside where DJ man's bottom pointing at ceiling. Mfanni does count - "One, two, three!" - and we start singing like those rap people on MTV:

> "African Queen and Kazakh Princess here, making all your troubles disappear!
>
> We rub-rub here and squeeze-squeeze there, Kleenex ready - we take good care!
>
> With magic hands and happy feet,
>
> Our musical show makes package complete! Happy ending guaranteed with flair,
>
> From Queen and Princess without compare!"

After our special performance (both singing and... other things), DJ man lying there with silly smile and what we call in homeland "sleeping soldier." He say, "Girls, you have rhythm!" trying to sound important.

"Yes," I say, "We know exactly who you are."

His face does that thing when balloon loses air. He try to escape but we keep him there, explaining very nice and sweet (but also bit threatening, like KGB) that we want free drinks and entry at Bedlam forever, or maybe his customers hear about his special love for my big toe.

Amazing how quick business deals happen when man is naked!

Later, walking home to my little room (which I make cozy with plastic flowers from pound shop), who appears like bad smell? PC Fuckwit the Clit! (This nickname I learn from Mfanni - is clever because he is both PC and... well, never mind). He been talking to sneaky Abdul again, asking about my activities of day.

I tell him straight: "Listen, Mr. Police Sir, you can have spies follow me like shadow, but if you want me spy for you, must let me do job. Is English saying - you scratch my front, I scratch your behind." (I think I mix this up but meaning is same).

He tries to be scary: "Don't play games or I shut down your massage place!" But I learn London ways now - his threats scary same as bunny wearing plastic vampire teeth.

Going to bed, brain is full of thoughts like busy beehive. We need Vertigo for security (and also because I maybe little bit like him now), but rent must be paid to mystery owner. And Clitter (ha! This nickname stick in head now) can make all the Dracula rabbit noises he wants - I do research in library (yes, they let anyone in!) and learn he cannot do much.

All this snake-piss (is good English word, no?) about framing me for Brady's heart explosion or stealing rubber balloons for willies... pah! Come do raid - what you find? Just lonely men getting happy endings. Not exactly crime of century, yes? Is why he want Vertigo so bad - bigger fish to catch than little massage girl from Zhanakorgan.

Fall into dream that taste like old vodka mixed with London fog...

...rain painting London streets in wobbly watercolors. I stick arm out for taxi - have been doing this for hours, or maybe years, time moving strange like drunk snail. In Zhanakorgan, you want transport, just whistle and magical goats with rainbow cart appear from thin air. Here? Cab drivers drift by like funeral boats, eyes sliding past me. Is like I wearing invisibility cloak from Harry Potter (which I read for English study - learn more about wands than proper grammar).

Finally, taxi emerge from fog like dream creature! But no - is stopping for tiny man who shrink and grow with each raindrop. When hat dissolve into mist, head shine brighter than all fires of Nauryz festival. Is Baldy Man. My stomach perform Olympic routine without proper training. Now he squats in back of brain like nomad who refuse leave winter camp in springtime.

Next day at work, trying to forget Chrome Dome, but brain not cooperate. Lucky first customer is football referee - very proper English gentleman until clothes come off. He bring special request: want me wear football boots while walking on his back. In my country, we have saying: man who ask for boots on back probably have story worth telling. He confess he referee women's football, want players to boss him around. Give big tip to keep secret from Gary Lineker (I think maybe this Gary is Queen's uncle? English celebrity system very confusing).

Business at Taban Bederi getting good - me and Mfanni becoming famous for four-hand special. Is like having reputation of best vodka maker in village, but less chance of going blind. Mfanni say we have USP - unique selling point. I think maybe she mean USB, like computer thing, but I not argue. English business terms more confusing than London Underground map.

We celebrate success in club called Bedlam where DJ keep calling us "beautiful bitches who work as witches." I want tell him witch in my country not sexy job - they curse cows and make milk turn sour. But Mfanni say all publicity good publicity, like all mushrooms good mushrooms (also not true - some mushrooms make you see dead relatives who still owe you money).

Men keep buying drinks, asking what we do. Some run away when we tell them, others try be sneaky, ask for number when friends not looking. Funny how London men brave only when nobody watching.

Next morning, head feeling like Russian shot-putter use it for practice, we find queue outside door longer than line for toilet at Glastonbury (English festival I hear about - sound like torture in field). Maybe we need bigger place. Maybe we need help. Maybe we need to stop drinking whiskey like it water.

London teaching me many things. Most important lesson: everyone here trying to act tough, but really, we all just trying to survive - some with football boots, some with badges, some with shiny heads. Is like big circus, but clowns all thinking they ringmaster.

CHAPTER 16

Going Mobile

So, Mr. Vertigo is not same man anymore. Gone is silly pimp who dress like rainbow threw up on him. Now he wear fancy suit and talk all serious-serious. Me and Mfanni meet him after workday that make my legs feel like overcooked kespe.

"My arms feel like I've been arm-wrestling entire bloody Arsenal!" Mfanni complain, doing silly flex pose.

"And my poor legs!" I say. "Is like doing Kazakh traditional dance all day, but without nice music!"

Mr. V (oh yes, he want fancy name now too) just give us look that make room feel cold. "No help for you two," he say, sipping tiny beer as if it's fancy champagne. "Time to move up in world.

Less work, more money. Quality over quantity, if your small brains can understand this concept."

We sit in Zig Zag club, but not in usual spot where music make ears bleed. No, we're in the corner, a proper business meeting. I look at customers, all sweaty and grabby with their pound notes, and suddenly they look... different. Village goats compared to city horses. Mfanni doing same thing - I see her nose go up like she smell bad fish. Funny how fast brain can change when money smell stronger than morals.

Mr. V looking proper English gentleman now - blue suit that probably cost more than my whole village, hair all neat with line cut in side that looks like mathematics equation. No more gold rings. Even his accent changing - less street, more BBC News.

"Ladies," he say, voice quiet, "tomorrow you have special appointment. Very special." He pause for drama effect, like bad Russian soap opera. "Eight hours with a gentleman client. In his private house."

Me and Mfanni sit there with mouths open, catching flies. Private house? In London, private house mean either very rich or very dodgy. Sometimes both.

Then come best part - or worst part, depending how you look at life. "Shaggy," he say to me, "this client knows you from Kazakhstan and wants you in traditional chapan."

I nearly fall off chair. "But traditional dress is back in Zhanakorgan! Cannot buy in Harrods unless they start selling clothes for Sheep Mating Festival!"

"Client provide clothes," he say, with smile that remind me of wolf from grandmother's stories.

Mfanni get jealous, like usual. "What about me? Why Miss Yurt-and- Camel getting special treatment?"

"Don't worry, princess," Mr. V say with smile that make my stomach do flip-flop, "he got plans for you too."

Next day, we in back of fancy car, driving through London that look more like fairy tale book - big houses hiding behind trees that probably older than my country. Giant metal monstergates open and we drive through to house that make Palace of Buckingham look like Moscow's worst Cosmos hotel.

I whisper to Mfanni, "This either best thing ever happen to us, or worst mistake since Great Grandfather try to sell Stalin used tractor." But Mr. V just tell me shut up in voice that make me wish I was back home herding goats.

Mfanni try comfort me, but I see her eyes meeting Mr. V eyes in mirror, doing secret dance of understanding that leave me out.

Not first time I feel like lamb being led to fancy butcher, but first-time butcher house look so expensive.

Welcome to London, where dreams come true... if you survive them first.

So, Mr. V stops car, and some fancy-pants man floats down steps like he's walking on clouds made of money. He does his quiet-talking thing with Mr. Fancy-Pants - probably discussing price of my soul or something equally cheerful. Next thing, me and Mfanni are told to follow this 'gentleman' (ha!) inside. Mfanni's there grinning like she just won lottery for free Botox, while I keep my face blank as a good Kazakh girl who's secretly planning escape route from shotgun wedding.

This 'gentleman' (who looks like he irons his underwear) leads us through doors that probably cost more than my whole village. Inside, we sit in room that makes my aunt's best carpet look like doormat.

When he leaves, I turn to Mfanni: "Listen here, you sneaky bitch, either tell me what's happening, or I start breaking things that look expensive!"

She gives me that 'calm down, stupid' look and whispers about money. Lots of money. So, I sit there trying to look calm while inside my head is screaming. All I can think is: 'Great, now I'm going to be fancy prisoner for rich English perverts who probably drink Earl Grey tea with their pinkies in the air while doing filthy things.'

After what feels enough time to milk whole herd of camels, in walks this tall man wearing white suit so bright it hurts my eyes. He's got hair like oil spill and beard that gets more attention than most babies.

"Good afternoon, ladies," he says, posh and proper. "I am Sheikh Ahmed bin Linah al Salaam, seventh richest man in England."

Oh, very nice. Why not just say 'I wipe my ass with hundred-pound notes'? Mfanni rolls her eyes so hard I think they might get stuck, and I keep face blank as brick.

Sheikh Moneybags catches Mfanni's eye-roll and says something about 'honesty in his culture.' Sure, and I'm Queen of England's favorite drinking buddy.

But then something weird happens - I start thinking he's not so bad. Even my nunu agrees, which is betrayal of highest order because nunu supposed to have better judgment.

He keeps talking with his fancy accent that sounds like honey being poured over gold bars: "You beautiful girls, I heard about your... skills. But I want something different."

My brain starts making emergency exit plans. How fast can I climb those gates? Can I use Mfanni as human shield?

But then Rich-Sheikh-Who-Reads-Minds says: "No no, I'm not English pervert! I'm Arab - we're very respectable! Just want something bit kinky for wealthy friends!"

He says 'kinky' as if its name of expensive French wine. Mfanni's already nodding yes, but I'm still suspicious like cat in room full of rocking chairs.

I interrupt their happy planning with: "We need rules." Because even in London, girl needs to protect her anoos from surprise attacks.

Money-Sheikh gets all cheerful: "Of course! No violence, no drugs, nothing illegal!" Well, that narrows it down to only about million possibilities.

Then comes talk about money - one thousand pounds per day just for staying in fancy prison, plus three thousand more after some party.

Mfanni practically faints from excitement. Me? I'm thinking this better not involve anything going where things shouldn't go.

Suddenly I'm feeling all warm and fuzzy. My ears are doing that thing where everything sounds like you're wrapped in expensive fur coat (not that I know what that feels like, but girl can dream).

I start thinking maybe this is it! My ticket to becoming Kazakh Princess of London! Then I can go back to Zhanakorgan and be proper queen - show those bitchy girls from school who used to laugh at my second- hand shoes who's boss now!

Sheikh Fancy-Pants claps his hands like he's summoning genie, and in walks Bernard, looking like penguin who got lost on way to posh restaurant. My jaw drops faster than camel with broken legs. He just grins.

CHAPTER 17

Bernard and the Mankini

One minute I am having nice warm fuzzy feelings like fresh goat milk on summer morning, next minute - poof! - all gone like when father's best horse ran away with village dowry.

"What the fuck is he doing here?" Mfanni says, showing exactly zero respect for penguin man. Sheikh just waves hand like he is brushing away fly from soup. "Bernard will make sure rules are followed," he says, then walks away speedier than my uncle Boltok running from angry wife.

Bernard tries to do his best soldier walk with stick up his ass. "Follow me," he says, and I think maybe stick really is up there. Mfanni leans close to my ear, her gold teeth catching light. "Don't worry babes, this little wanker couldn't scare a baby mouse. I could put him on his back and piss on him easy."

Bernard's ears must be better than village gossip woman because he spins around, face all twisted like he ate bad kebab. "Save that for your clients." Ha! Not what he was saying few weeks ago when Mfanni was giving him special attention under table at club. But I keep mouth shut tight like grandmother's purse strings.

He lead us down corridor that shine brighter than Sheikh's collection of gold teeth. Every few steps he stop to point at different doors - "This massage room, this steam room, this place where rich people pay to sit in hot rocks like lizard on vacation." Finally, he open last door, give us look that say "behave or else" (but we remember what his "or else" mean from club incident), then disappear quicker than last dumpling at family dinner.

Then comes funny part - we end up in fancy room with bubble bath that Mfanni calls "jacuzzi." Before I can say "wawaweewa," she is naked and splashing around like happy seal. "Get your yellow ass in here!" she shouts. "My black one is lonely!" This makes me giggle like schoolgirl, and I think maybe one thousand pounds per day not so bad for playing in fancy bath.

For few beautiful minutes, life is perfect. We float in magic bubbles like queens of England, except more naked and with better jokes. Mfanni show me how to make water shoot from special holes - aim just right and can hit ceiling! Is moment of pure joy, like finding extra meat in beshbarmak.

But then Bernard bursts in without knock, like KGB in old country. He has bag with "costumes" - if you can call dirty rags costumes. Mfanni gets one that looks like something even my brother would refuse to wear. I get... pink mankini. Yes, like my brother Borat's famous swimming suit.

This little bald bastard has done research better than university professor! He knows my family secret!

Mfanni refuses to wear rag (good for her!), so Bernard pulls out taser. What the fuck! ZAP! Down goes Mfanni, titties flying everywhere like pole dancer who lose grip during final act. I stand there thinking this definitely not in massage therapist job description.

Then things get weird. Bernard starts getting... excited. Very excited. He's touching himself through pants while I'm standing there in mankini that's made for man parts, not lady parts. Very awkward!

But then I see opportunity better than black market toilet paper deal. I start talking mean to Bernard, and he gets more excited than pig in mud. Me and Mfanni (who wakes up mad as bear) decide to teach him lesson. Next thing, Mfanni sitting on his face while he does weird dance on floor. Is like traditional Kazakh wrestling match, but much more disturbing.

When Sheikh calls us for dinner over fancy speakers (rich people have voices in walls!), he tries to make joke about Kazakh food ("horse d'oeuvres"). He thinks he's very clever, but I've heard better ones from village drunk who thinks he's married to turnip.

CHAPTER 18

Albasty

R ich men never stop coming! Line of fancy cars outside longer than queue for last toilet paper during Covid lockdown. Bernard being extra nice now - too nice, like snake offering apple in garden. Something about his smile make me nervous, but what can I do?

He bring rich customers, steady stream like water from broken tap. Our special service stays same though - me walking on customers with my feet (very professional), and Mfanni doing her thing with their... how you say... private matters.

One evening, we're having nice dinner with Sheikh - proper beshmarek and shorpa, just like mama used to make but more fancy. Sheikh starts talking about "extra work". I'm thinking, why bother? My post office account already has twenty thousand British pounds! But Mfanni, she gets dollar signs in eyes like when Almaty pickpocket spots tourist wallet. "We must do it!" she says. Stupid, greedy woman.

"Very, very special guest," Sheikh says, like he's selling magic carpet. Then he tells us about some war hero with "post dramatic dress disorder" (whatever fancy English words mean) who needs "special therapy." When Sheikh tells us money amount, I think maybe my ears are broken like old Soviet radio. But there's always catch, yes? As we say back home: "When wolf offers free meat, check if your legs still attached."

Sheikh just stares at me when I say this, not friendly as usual. More like angry goat before it headbutts you. So, I do what good Kazakh wife does - shut mouth, nod head, pretend everything perfectly normal. Ha! Nothing normal about any of this.

Later, Bernard gives me black plastic mankini that makes me look like confused seal at circus. Mfanni gets sexy jungle outfit with bouncy parts showing - of course she does! She gets to look like goddess, I look as if someone wrapped trash bag around boiled potato. London fashion makes no sense.

Then comes Mr. Smith. Oh, Mr. Smith! If boring was person, it would be jealous of this man. So average, so normal, vanilla yogurt wearing suit. But his eyes... Albasty! The devil himself! Back home, grandmother warned about such things. Should have listened to grandmother more, less to Radio Eurasia's "Top Hundred Songs About Heroic Tractor Drivers."

Everything goes to shit faster than camel can spit. Mfanni disappears - poof! - leaving me alone with this demon in man costume. He speaks Kazakh (of course demon speaks Kazakh, why not?), pulls out his kamcha, and... well, let's say now my behind look like map of Soviet Union during height of communism - all red with painful borders.

Later, I'm sitting in red jacuzzi water (not good kind of red), and Bernard comes in screaming about cleaning. Mfanni finally shows up to defend me - bit late, dear friend! I want to call her bad names, but my brain hurts more than my... damaged areas.

Sheikh gives us "bonus" money as if it makes everything okay. Five thousand pounds to forget devil man with whip - London prices for pain very strange! Vertigo drives us home, acting like we just had spa day instead of horror show.

Back in my little Bush room, Landlordlady hugs me into her giant bosoms - like being suffocated by warm, perfume-smelling pillow fort. Feels safe. Maybe this is what London teaching me: sometimes comfort comes in strange places, and memories fade but scars make good stories. Just maybe not stories to tell mama back home.

At least post-office account getting fat. In Za, we say money doesn't buy happiness, but in London, it buys better quality nightmares.

CHAPTER 19

The Cloud of the Silver Lining

B ack home, we have saying: "When wallet gets fat, soul gets skinny." True, twenty thousand British pounds now sit in my account, but my heart feels heavier than grandmother's special dumplings.

I try to find someone to blame. Maybe Mfanni? She use me like fancy decoration in shop window - "Come see exotic Kazakh girl! Sister of famous Borat!" But no, she also good friend.

Then there is V. In my village, even snake has more honor than him. He takes big money from Sheikh for driving us around like fancy cattle, probably same amount as we get for having our dignity surgically removed. Proper bastard, as British people say - though I never understand this. In Kazakhstan, all bastards are improper, that's whole point.

I'm alone now because Mfanni flies to Jamaica like rich tourist (say she need to "sort out business with cousin who run beach bar" - but I think cousin probably six feet tall with muscles like Olympic athlete).

London street feels different when walking alone - like sheep separated from flock, except probably get less pervert looks (except in Betpak-Dala steppe, but that story best left for long winter night).

I go to open Taban Bederi, and who do I find waiting there? Constable Clitter! But no funny hat today - he wearing normal clothes like spy in bad movie.

"Hey, Officer Clitter!" I say. "You playing dress-up today?" He calls me "stupid Kazakh cow" which makes my blood boil like samovar someone accidentally put on nuclear reactor. I'm thinking maybe I start calling him "stupid British pig" - see how he like taste of his own food (or is it medicine) that make cardboard look exciting.

Then comes funny part. I tell him about Sheikh's house, about Mfanni getting tasered like Christmas turkey and me getting whipped like cart horse. His mouth opens wider than village drunk at free bar. He wants proof, so I take him inside shop. Big mistake, like letting wolf guard have password to sheep's dating app.

"Show me evidence," he says, trying to sound professional like doctor who didn't buy degree from back of magazine. I start removing clothes slowly (because my ass still feeling like it got kissed by angry bear), and suddenly Officer Clitter becomes very interested in "thorough investigation."

Next thing I know, his finger is exploring my backside like he looking for lost treasure. I jump up like spooked horse. "Congratulations, Officer!" I say. "You just left fingerprints on my ass and DNA where sun never shines! What will your boss think about THIS evidence?"

He runs away quicker than my brother when woman says "marriage," shouting about filing report. Ha! In my country, we say man who invades bottom has no moral high ground.

I keep Taban Bederi open by myself now. Things different without Mfanni - have to do more than foot walking. Few weeks ago, I would rather milk angry bull than do these things. Now? Is just Tuesday. Money keeps coming, no more whips or tasers or crazy men in boring suits. Maybe this is what British people call "professional development."

Mfanni calls from Jamaica, says she meets man with big car (we know what that means - compensation for small tractor.) She's staying there, leaving me alone in London like last potato at potato famine.

My bumcheek scars heal but still see, bad memories written in flesh. In mirror, they tell story - "Welcome to London, where dreams come true but leave marks." British people say every cloud has silver lining. But in my life, silver lining has cloud, cloud has silver lining, and everything spinning like washing machine filled with broken dreams and cheap vodka. Is cosmic comedy where universe play joke, and I am punchline.

Maybe this is growing up, London style. Or maybe is just life teaching lesson: in big city, everyone gets scars - some you can see, some you can't, and some you only show to police officers who forget they are police officers.

At least I have money for nice clothes now. Can walk around London like Kazakh Princess - though nobody notice difference between princess and massage girl. Is funny thing about London - everyone too busy looking at phone to see person right in front of them, even if person is wearing crown made from post office savings account.

CHAPTER 20

Pidjondars Come Home to Roost

Life was becoming very nice and cozy. My business? Good! My bum? No longer looking like baboon's red face after healing! My Bush home? Perfect! So, I decide to do what smart person does - forget all bad things from past. But silly me forgets one very important lesson from old Kazakh saying: just because you forget past doesn't mean past forgets to bite you in ass.

I'm getting quite happy forgetting about Sheikh (may camel spit in his tea), Vertigo (may his balls shrivel like raisins), Mfanni (actually, I miss her), and PC Clitter (may he step in dog shit). The less I think of these arseholes, the more my life feels like sweet kumis on summer day.

Then - BOOM! - like thunder from clear sky, fucking Bernard waddles into my Taban Bederi! I thought the greasy little bald pidjondar had flown away when Sheikh didn't need his sneaky ass anymore. But no - here he is, standing in my doorway with smile that doesn't reach eyes, like chess player who already see ten moves ahead.

"You have balls size of watermelon coming here, Bernard!" I shout at him. "Maybe you want special treatment? I give you massage you never forget - with baseball bat!" But he just pushes past me like man who know exactly where he going, into my treatment room.

Then he drops bomb bigger than ones Americans drop in movies: "Sheikh fired me. I want to work for you now." His voice too smooth, like oil on water. Something in way he say it make skin crawl. Ha! I laugh in his face. "Trust you? Bernard, you are more slippery than greased pig at village festival. You couldn't even lie straight in coffin!"

But then he tells me something that makes my stomach feels like I swallowed angry hedgehog: "They're coming for you. Think your cutting into their business and know too much, playing footsie with the cops and stitching up Vertigo." His eyes watching me whole time, measure me like scientist with experiment going exactly as planned.

And who is THEY? The Sheik and his friends?

Fuck-fuck-fuck! Not normal kind of fuck like tired-fuck or sexy-times-fuck, but special kind of fuck that means I'm in deeper shit than a one-armed man in quicksand.

He also tells me Clitter has Vertigo in handcuffs and wants me to do court testimony thing - you know, hand on holy book, tell truth, whole truth, nothing but truth bollocks. Not good situation for girl from steppes, I tell you!

So what do I do? I make Bernard my assistant! Yes, yes, I know - like making fox guard chicken house. But sometimes in London, you need rat to catch bigger rat. Besides, he now scared of mystery people too, so we're both swimming in same shit-creek without paddle.

We move to new flat in place called Elephant's Castle (English people very strange with names). Two bedrooms, thank fuck - I rather kiss camel bottom than share bed with Bernard. But now I have bigger problem: visa running out faster than sheep running from horny shepherd. Soon I be illegal immigrant - another pidjondar coming home to shit on my head.

And here I sit in Flying Tishkan, watching Bernard try to eat sorpa like proper person instead of English twat he is. Those fake Russki-Kazakhs at other tables laughing - they think I've gone from strong black woman to little bald man. But they don't know my clever plan. In London, I learn fast - sometimes you need snake to catch bigger snake. And Bernard? He's my little snake now. Or at least I think he is

As I watch him choke on proper Kazakh food (ha!), I think maybe London teaching me too well. Before, I was nice girl who smile and be polite. Now I know - in this city, to get respect you must give shit first, or shit comes to you. Well, at least I learning something useful, yes?

CHAPTER 21

The Pelvic Floor

So, big news from London - I am becoming specialist service provider for rich men with too much money and too little shame. Yes, yes, I know what I said before about never doing this, but what choice I have? No Mfanni, no proper job, no working papers, and visa looking more expired than last week's kurt. I need money fast, so I use what God give me - my hands. Well mostly now my feet. I could say I am top escort in all Kazakhstan, but this is like saying you have cleanest toilet in bus station - maybe true, maybe not, who care? Important thing is, I keep standards. No funny business in my special places. My flower garden is closed for visitors, if you know what I mean. I not going back to homeland looking like I been hosting Olympic Games down there!

Walking Knightsbridge Street, thinking of business plans like proper London entrepreneur. Weather here is devil's armpit - cold, wet, making me sneeze. And every time I sneeze... ai-ya- yai... let's just say my body betraying me worse than corrupt government official. My down-below muscles weak like old babushka's handshake, thanks to thing that happened in Zhanakorgan. But this story is for another time when vodka is stronger, and night is longer.

Get taxi to my fancy apartment in Elephant Castle (still have not seen elephant, or castle - London full of lies).
Bernard waiting there with new client, some fancy-pants lord from gentleman's club.

"Lapshagul, meet Lord Teverson," Bernard says, voice too

polished, too rehearsed. "He write book about Central Asia, wants to interview you... closely." His eyes gleam with calculation that make me nervous. I almost laugh teeth out, but notice how Bernard watching us both like spider counting flies in web.

They sit on my white sofa (very expensive, very clean, for now). I look at Lord what's-his-face and say, "How close this interview need to be, Lordy? We talking Wikipedia close or National Geographic close?" His face go red like sunset over Astana.

Price agreed (very nice, very, very nice), and I take him to special room. Lights low, music soft. I tell him lay down, crack knuckles like I about to wrestle bear. "Ready for traditional Kazakh massage? Very famous!

Poor Lordy looking nervous now, mumbling something about "academic research" - ha! Academic research my aunt's moustache! I climb on back, push hands like I kneading dough for world's biggest baursak. "This special technique called Strong Woman Fingers of Steppe," I tell him. "Good for stress, better for making man appreciate simple things, like having working spine."

Everything going fine, I'm doing eagle dance on his back, singing old village song about brave warrior who slip on cow pat, when disaster strike - ACHOO! And with sneeze comes shame. Warm shame. Right there, all over distinguished English lord's back.

His body freeze like Lake Balkhash in winter. "Everything okay?" he ask with posh squeaky voice full of worry.

Quick thinking needed! "Is special treatment!" I practically yell. "Very exclusive! Called Golden Blessing of Steppe! Only for most honored clients!"

"Golden... Blessing?" he say, voice wobbly now.

"Yes! Very rare! Very expensive! You lucky man - others wait years for this treatment!" I jump off his back like it suddenly catch fire, grab towel, wipe him down more careful than KGB agent cleaning crime scene.

He pay extra (guilt money, I think) and leave quick. I tell Bernard, who waiting in living room like nosy neighbor, "This city will kill me dead." Then I sneeze again. "Blyad!"

Why you dancing like you need toilet?" Bernard ask, stupid as day is long. I show him why by giving his face intimate meeting with my wet underwear. "Agh! You're a crazy woman!" he shout as he jumped back, but I see his eyes get that look. No thank you - last thing I need is excited Bernard trying to play his love song on my expensive sofa. Some things even Golden Blessing can't fix.

Is funny thing, but after this I am thinking like maybe me and Mfanni doing massage with two hands, two feet being golden ticket, this another one of those possible USBs?

Very important in London, having something special that other people not having. So, I tell Bernard, who suddenly look less like pervert and more like accountant counting profits, "Darling Bernard, you go to bathroom now, clean up greasy ass and go back to fancy club and bring me steady supply of these fancy Lords."

But his eyes are not foggy like usual - instead they sharp, calculating, like man who just found golden key. "Bernard! You listen or just play with yourself?" He stay quiet, face blank but mind clearly working overtime behind those beady eyes. So I grab him like kindergarten teacher catch teenager reading "Плейбой Россия" and march him to bathroom.

Later, when he finish getting respectable, I tell him again, and off he go like good puppy dog.

Two in morning (London never sleep, like disease of insomniyah), I hear voices in flat. Is Bernard, drunk, with another man holding him up. "This belong to you?" ask man, pointing at Bernard hanging like wet clothes on washing line. "Unfortunately, yes," I say, feeling annoyed. "Just drop him anywhere on floor."

"I'm perfeshly fine!" Bernard say with tongue that seem too big for mouth. "Lapshagul, thish is Mishter Tarquin Napper, Immigration Shecretary." I say "Hello" with mouth, but brain say "Jackpot!" I know opportunity when it knock, even if knock sound like drunk Bernard falling on floor.

Minister Napper eye me up and down like karaan. "Bernard said, when he could still talk proper English, that you do special a very special Kazakh massage. Is this perhaps a good time now?"

"Minister! Of course is good time!" I say with smile big like Caspian Sea. "You come for special traditional healing? Perfect! You look like man who shout too much in big government building, yes? Need relax treatment?"

He agree, say something about hard week, heard about "unique services." His face go pink like baby pig. I clap hands like excited seal. "Yes! I am best Kazakh healer in all South London! My techniques make history! Take off clothes, lie on bed. I make you feel like stallion!"

He look nervous, check room with squinty eyes, but start taking off clothes, fold them neat-neat like origami. In underwear only, he get on bed, mumbling about "keeping it professional." I laugh. "Always professional, Minister! Like BBC!"

Then massage begin. I poke his back like scientist studying specimen. "This tension from telling too many government lies, yes?" He make nervous laugh, jump when I push harder. "Something like that."

I jump on his back like mounting prize stallion. "This special technique - Ride of Steppe Warrior. Very ancient, very sacred."

He make noise like stepped-on cat. "Quite... intense," he say through teeth.

"Intense is good!" I say, now really getting into role. "Is how we remove government corruption from body!" I start singing old Kazakh song about brave warrior who lose way in snowstorm, very loud.

I feel sneeze coming on like winter storm, trying to hold back for extra drama effect, but like trying to stop avalanche with umbrella until....

......ACHOO!

And then... BA-BAKH...my special problem happens, the one doctor claim needs a fancy-pants exercise, but now my USB superpower!

Warm feeling spread like spring thaw.

"What in God's name?!" Minister shout.

"Congratulations, Minister! You receive most sacred Kazakh blessing - Golden Shower of Steppe!" He turn head like owl. "Golden what?"

"Golden Shower of Steppe!" I say again, proud like mother showing off ugly baby. "Very powerful! Only for most important men. In my country, this mean great success coming! Very expensive treatment!" He blink many times... "That's... certainly different."

I clean him up with towel, explaining whole time about ancient wisdom and power of treatment. He keep saying must be very discrete, no one know.

"Of course, Minister," I say, trying not to laugh. "Kazakh healer like priest - everything stay secret. Even when you smell like wet blanket tomorrow, no one know why!"

He leave looking confused, but many pounds on table. I think maybe London teaching me too well - starting to think like crafty fox instead of simple village girl. But crafty fox eat better than honest sheep, this I learn quick in big city.

CHAPTER 22

The Curious Case of the Tesco Bag

So let me tell you, dear readers, about new reality of Lapshagul, proud daughter of Kazakh steppes, former masseuse, now accidental dominatrix who has come, like when bowl of kumis turns into Samruk cognac in middle of family dinner.

Sometimes I am thinking this London town has been given some magic potion of madness. Back in my village, if I would tell anyone these stories, they would think I was having possession by shaitans or eating too much fermented mare's milk.

The rich and powerful men here? They are begging for pain, humiliation, and sometimes even their own death—but only if it is stylish and given by yours truly.

As always, these stories are starting with Bernard, my bald, supposedly devoted little house slave. Bernard always have way of making things happen - too many things, now that I think about it. One minute I'm drowning like rat in deep river, next —boom! Door swings open like magic. Like I had invisible hand pushing me forward, and Bernard always there, pulling strings I cannot see.

Sometimes late at night, after too much vodka, I wonder if maybe Bernard not just helpful pervert - if maybe he have plan behind those watery eyes. But then I think - ha! This is crazy talk, like when grandmother think neighbor's cow plotting against her.

The humiliation not my idea—he insist on it. For what seem

endless variations, he helps me to find wealthy clients who want to experience "Kazakh domination," as he is so dramatically calling it.

I am laughing every time I hear it. What is Kazakh domination? In home, women don't dominate! We cannot even raise our voices. It is men who rule the yurt and sometimes knock their wives over head with yak leg bone if dinner is late. Women like me were supposed to get water, cook baursaks, and quietly endure. Yet here I am, queen of Elephant and Castle, holding whip instead of teapot.

On with story. Bernard told me he has found client from Parliament. Very rich, respectable man. "He pays well," Bernard said with that naughty glint in his eye. I thought, why not? I am not one to be afraid of good payday. The man arrives, and must say, he is handsome, proper English gentleman with angel face, no older than thirty. Real Prince Charming— until he opens mouth.

He gives me Tesco bag. I thought, Oh, how nice, he brought me little snack! Maybe biscuits? Sandwich? I smiled and said, "You did not have to bring me anything."

But no. He looked me in eyes—blue eyes that could make butter melt— and said with most serious face, "It is my dog's poop."

Poop!?

I became like statue. Back home, we use cow dung for making fires and frying baursaks, those delicious little doughnuts. My first thought was, "Should I fry baursaks for this man in yard?" But before I could ask, he fell to knees, grabbed my boots, and declared, "My mistress, punish me properly!"

Now, in home, if man would kneel before woman, village would gossip for months. His family would do shamanic intervention to clean the shame. Here, this handsome Englishman was now begging me to make him eat dog poop.

And that was not all—oh no. He brought dishwasher tablets and bottle of Fairy dish soap. "Make me eat these," he said, holding them up like gifts to cruel goddess. "Make me drink your urine from toilet. Step on my stomach in heels. Poison me, mistress. I am ready to die at your hands."

My first thought was to slap him to his senses. So, I took my favorite whip—Kazakh leather, strong and never forgiving—and started beating him. Hard. Each crack of whip made echo through yard of Elephant and Castle. I thought, This will make his shaitans leave for sure.

He made pathetic little moan. "Thank you, mistress! More, please!"

What kind of men are these ones? In Kazakhstan, if man would dare ask wife to step on his stomach in heels, she would think he lost his mind.

Neighbors would say, "Shaman must burn sheep brain for him." Here, in London, they give you big money for this madness. I should send some of this money to my village, let women see how tables have turned around.

When I finished with him, he was lying on floor, with happy smile on angel face. "You are incredible," he whispered. "A goddess."

I told him, "I am Borat's crazy sister, but not that crazy. If you want to die, find other dominatrix. I like customers who come back."

Bernard, who was hiding behind door like always, watching everything with those clever little eyes, made big laugh when man left. "You are natural, Lapshagul," he said, wiping tears from eyes that never quite match his laughter.

I shook my head. In home, this man would be sent to mountains to herd yak until he remembered how to be proper man. Here, they fall at my feet with Tesco bags of dog poop.

So here I am, Lapshagul, accidental dominatrix, cultural ambassador of steppes. Who knew my ancestors' skills with whips and dung fires would one day make me rich person? Life is strange thing, my friends. Strange and full of surprises.

CHAPTER 23

Findom

A nd another, Bernard telling me he have something very interesting to tell me. He say, "Lapshagul, we have new client coming for Findom. He is no ordinary man—he is Minister of Finance of some small European country. Imagine, man who controls entire nation's treasury wants you to control his personal wallet. Think how funny, Lapshagul!" Bernard slapped his bald head, laughing, but I thought, "This is strange. In Zhaṇakorgan, we do not allow anyone to rob us unless they are the government. And even then, we don't call it robbery, we call it 'tradition.'"

When Minister arrived, I was confused. He was small, round, and looked like dumpling that had been left in stewpot too long. His suit was shiny, like he borrowed it from game show host. He bowed deeply and said, "Mistress Lapshagul, I am here to surrender everything to you."

"Everything?" I asked, narrowing eyes. "Does this mean your wife too? Your Rolls Royce? Your best pair of socks?"

"No, Mistress," he said, shaking head nervously. "Only my money. Empty my accounts. I want you to take everything. Bernard says you are best in London."

I gave Bernard side-eye. "Why you are promising these men so much, Bernard? If he has no money left, how will he pay for my next massage table?"

Bernard only smirked, his bald head glistening like onion in market, and something flicker behind his eyes - calculating look that disappear so fast maybe I imagine it. "You'll see, Lapshagul," he said, voice smooth like expensive vodka. "This one is different. He wants to suffer, and suffering pays." Way he say it make me wonder if he collecting more than just money from these men. But maybe London paranoia getting to me - when you live in city this crazy, everything start looking like conspiracy.

Session begin. "You call yourself Minister of Finance, but you have no dignity. You want me to rob you like bandit in hills of Zhanakorgan? Very well, I will do it, but only because I am generous!" I waved my kamcha dramatically, and he whimpered like kid goat tied to tree.

"Tell me your bank account number," I demanded.

He hesitated, looking at me with big, wet eyes. "I... I don't remember it, Mistress."

"You don't remember? Are you Minister or donkey?!" I shouted, cracking kamcha against carpet. He squealed and pulled out his phone to check his banking app for number. These Europeans, so weak. In my country, even children know their bank details by heart—mostly so they can hide their money from uncles.

When he finally gave me number, I made big show of transferring his money. I shouted random Kazakh words like "Shashlyk!" and "Kumis bilezik!" to make it sound mystical and terrifying. In reality, I was using Bernard's laptop - funny how he always have exactly right tools at exactly right time. Screen full of viruses, like Zhanakorgan hospital during flu season, but maybe that not only thing hidden in computer. I didn't take his money, but I let him believe I did. Later, catch Bernard typing away on same laptop, fingers moving quick like spider weaving web. When I ask what he doing, he close screen faster than politician hiding tax papers. But maybe I seeing things that not there - too much time in London make everyone bit crazy, yes?

"Now you are poor," I told him. "You have nothing left. How does it feel to be like Kazakh villager during tax season?"

"It feels... liberating, Mistress," he whispered, tears streaming down face.

"Good. Now go buy me new pair of shoes with money I didn't take," I ordered. He nodded eagerly and scurried away, leaving his dignity behind like old pair of socks.

After he left, Bernard and I sat down to count actual money he had paid just for this session. "This is ridiculous," I said, shaking head. "In Zhanakorgan, if someone asked me to rob them, I would laugh and tell them to go to Ministry of Internal Affairs. That is where real professionals are."

"But you are professional now, Lapshagul," Bernard said, pouring himself cup of tea. "You are not just woman from Zhanakorgan anymore. You are Borat's sister, greatest findom queen in London."

I thought about this. Maybe Bernard was right. Maybe I am queen. Or maybe I am just very good at pretending. Either way, as long as they keep paying, I will keep swinging my kamcha.

CHAPTER 24

Slave of the White Panties

Should I continue? I know, is not part of story, but must tell you men here... pfft... such strange creatures. Is like animal show on TV, but animals wear fancy scarf in summer heat and say sorry to lamp post when walking into it.

Take this man, for example. Normal looking, works for oil company. Very polite, very intelligent. Wears suit that cost more than tractor. But he has one weakness: white panties. First time he came to me; I thought he made joke.

"I am your slave," he said, bowing low like I am Queen of World.

"Just say words: white panties, and I will do anything."

At first, I thought, maybe he is confused. Maybe in Britain, "white panties" means "hello" or "thank you." But no, he explained everything with detail. Too much detail. I almost dropped my kamcha.

"You mean," I asked, trying for understanding, "if I say white panties, you become like sheep? Bahhh, bahhh?"

"Yes," he said, looking very serious. "A sheep, your slave sheep."

I laughed so hard I spilled my tea. In Zhanakorgan, men are strong, proud, and stubborn like donkeys. They torture wives with chores, with yelling, with too much vodka. And they do it for free! But this British man, he pays me—pays me much money —to be tortured. What strange country.

First time he brought his own tools, I was confused. He opened big leather bag, and out came ropes, clamps, blindfolds, and something that looked like small paddle for punishing naughty children.

"You carry this bag to work?" I asked him.

"No, no," he said, becoming red. "This is just for... personal use."

I shook head. In Zhanakorgan, if man carries bag like this, he is chased from village. In London, they call him "executive."

"Okay," I said, picking up my kamcha. "We begin your torture, Kazakh style. Take off shirt."

He obeyed, of course. He is my sheep slave of white panties.

First time, I try gentle. Small slap here, tiny pokey-poke there. But he keep saying, 'Harder! More!' So I give him true Kazakh experience. I swing kamcha same way grandfather taught me for stubborn donkey, same way we chase chicken from grandmother's potatoes.

Whack! Whack! He make noise of baby goat, but face shows... happiness? "You are okay?" I asked.

"Never better," he said, like grinning boy who steals first look at neighbor's daughter through crack in yurt flap.

One time, he came twice in week. I told him, "You know, in my country, if you visit woman this much, you must marry her."

He laughed and said, "But I'm already married!"

"Your wife knows you here?" I asked, raising eyebrow.

"No, no," he said quickly. "She thinks I'm at business meeting."

Ah, British men and their secrets. In Zhanakorgan, if man lies to wife, she knows right away. Kazakh women have sixth sense. Also, we smell vodka on breath.

One day, I decided for asking him. "Why you like this? Why you pay so much money to be tortured?"

He thought for moment, then said, "Because, in my real life, I'm boss. I give orders. Everyone respects me, but no one challenges me. Here, with you, I don't have to be in charge. I can let go."

This made me think. Back in home, men never want to "let go." They hold onto pride, power, vodka bottles. But here in London, men pay to feel powerless. To feel weak. It is strange, but also... maybe it makes sense?

After he left, I sat in fancy flat and thought about my life. In Zhanakorgan, I never imagined I would be here, in big city, hitting rich men with kamcha and making more money in week than most people make in year. Back home, people would call me crazy. But here, I am successful. I am businesswoman. I give these men what they want, and they pay me for it.

Still, I miss some things about Kazakhstan. Mountains, fresh air, way people tell truth even when it hurts. Here in London, everything is lie. Even landmarks. No elephant. No castle. But there is me, Lapshagul, with my kamcha, my USB, and Kazakh spirit. And as long as British men have strange desires and big wallets, I will be here, making them squeal like piglets.

Kazakhstan is strange, London is stranger, and I am somewhere in middle.

CHAPTER 25

Dog Slave

A nd finally....

Aslan stood before me, this towering young millionaire who had conquered the Forbes list before the age of 30. Yet, here he was, on the floor of my flat, groveling like guilty puppy caught chewing best Turkish carpet. His expensive cologne mixed oddly with the scent of desperation-very nice actually!

"Mistress," he begged, "please abuse me. I am a bad dog."

I stood there, stunned, clutching my bottle of Shubat (fermented camel milk-very good constitutional) for courage. In my Kazakh homeland, a man falling at a woman's feet only happens if he's been drinking too much kumis and can't stand up. Here in London, it seems men do it on purpose. What a land of strange rituals!

"Wait," I said, pointing at him with my besik taspa.

"What is this 'dog slave'? Kazakh dogs are respected members of the household. They guard our yurts and herd our animals. Are you saying I should treat you like naughty sheepdog? Do you want me to tie you to a tree outside and throw old baursaks at you?"

"Yes, Mistress," Aslan whimpered, his face lighting up with hope. "Exactly like that."

I blinked. "And you are millionaire? You built your empire from nothing? How? By crawling into business meetings on all fours, barking for investors?"

"No, Mistress," he said, looking confused. "I am very professional in business. But in private, I... I like to surrender. Please, punish me."

Ah, the irony. In my country, men punish women for everything: cooking the beshbarmak wrong, having girl baby instead of boy, or daring to speak mind. But here? Rich Western men pay good money for women to humiliate them. It's like world has turned upside down. My brother Borat was right—these Westerners are insane.

"Well," I said, cracking my knuckles, "you have come to the right place. In my country, we have many traditional punishments. Let's see how much of a bad dog you really are."

I grab a wooden kazan spoon from the kitchen. "This is for stirring goat head soup," I explained, waving it at him. "But tonight, it will be for stirring sense into you. Now crawl!"

Aslan dropped to his hands and knees, wagging an imaginary tail. "Yes, Mistress! Woof, woof!"

"Good," I say with devil smile. "First, we test loyalty. A dog must prove it worthy of the family. Fetch!" I threw one of my old tastiks (embroidered pillows) across room. Aslan scampered after it, his designer shoes squeaking on the floor. He grabs it in his teeth and brings it back, looking up at me like a proud golden retriever.

"Not bad," I said, trying not to laugh. "But loyalty not enough. We value strength, most important. If a dog cannot protect the herd, it is useless. Now, you must wrestle me!"

His eyes widen like full moon. "Mistress, are you serious?"

"Of course! In my village, women wrestle men all the time. How else do you think we survive marriage?"

I grabbed his arm and twisted it behind his back. He yelping baby

89

noise, clearly not used to being manhandled by a woman from Zhanakorgan. Pin him to floor faster than grandmother make baursak.

"Pathetic," I said. "If you were a Kazakh man, your ancestors would die from shame twice. Now bark like real dog!"

"Woof, woof!" he cried, his face pressed into the carpet.

"Louder!" I demanded. "In Kazakhstan, wolves must hear you from miles away."

"WOOF! WOOF!" His voice echoed through the apartment.

I was starting to enjoy myself. Who knew that tormenting rich British men could be such good therapy? But then I remembered Bernard's words about that secret forum. What if these men were writing reviews of me? What if my name became famous as the "Kazakh Mistress of Elephant and Castle"?

I paused. Should I be ashamed? Should I be insulted? But then think of all the women back home who had suffered in silence. If I could mock and humiliate just one powerful man, wasn't that a small victory for sisters?

I looked down at Aslan, panting like a tired Tobet. "You did well," I said, patting his head with the kazan spoon. "But next time, bring proper gift. In my country, when a man begs for mercy, he must bring a chicken or a bag of flour. Otherwise, how will the woman feed her family?"

"Yes, Mistress," Aslan said eagerly. "I will bring you whatever you want. Just name it."

I smirked. "Very well. Next time, bring me... a yurt in Mayfair."

And with that, I kicked him out of my apartment, feeling both confused and oddly triumphant. The Kazakhs have a saying: "If you cannot kill your enemy, make them carry your water." Tonight, I made a millionaire bark like a dog. Close enough.

As I locked the door, I poured myself a glass of Shubat and toasted to my newfound career. Borat may embarrass our country, but his sister? She will conquer the UK, one dog slave at a time.

As I drink my shubat and watch London lights through window, think maybe Western decadence not so bad after all. At least here, woman can be boss - even if must pretend to be dominatrix to do it. Is like father always say: "In life, must sometimes milk bull to get cream." Never understand what he mean until now.

Tomorrow will buy new whip from pet shop. Maybe even learn proper English words for domination. But for now, just enjoy victory and plan how to get that Mayfair yurt. London property market very expensive - must milk many rich bulls to afford!

CHAPTER 26

Dealing with Pigeons

A nd now back to regular scheduled program!

Coming out from Harrods "Cut Price" Outlet (which is not real Harrods, by the way - very sneaky English trick), arms full with shopping, I see them.

Standing there like two evil statues made of bad intentions - Vertigo and Mfanni! Fifty meters away but their eyes burning holes in me like laser beams from James Bond film. My brain suddenly goes 'ding!' - of course they work together!

They start walking towards me, moving like angry bears who just found someone stealing honey. In my village, we have saying: "When bears come for honey, smart person climbs highest tree." London has no trees, but thank Allah, it has black taxi! I jump inside. "Go, go! Elephant's Castle!" I scream, leaving them standing there with faces like they just ate very bad curry.

At apartment, what do I find? Bernard, spread on sofa like sad naked starfish, thinking he will get lucky. Ha! I tell him, "Put clothes on, you desperate English pervert! We have emergency more important than your lonely penis!" After I tell him about Vertigo and Mfanni situation, something change in his face - like mask slipping for second before he catch it. Then he gets serious, though eyes still hungry when looking at me.

My situation now more complicated than Brexit (which I still not understand - why leave Europe when Europe has best prostitutes?). People want to kill me, police no good because

Detective Clitter probably wants to arrest me or worse, and only friend I have is Bernard, who acts devoted like puppy but sometimes watch me with eyes too sharp for simple pervert. Plus, my visa running out faster than toilet paper in curry house. But then - BOOM! - genius idea hits me like drunk driver in Moscow.

I give Bernard special mission. He agrees too quick, but want... how you say... favor first. Ai-yi-yi! What I do for this favor make village grandmother roll in grave so fast she could power small city. But survival in London more important than dignity - this I learn very quick, like tourist learning to avoid eye contact on Underground.

Bernard brings Lord Blithering back to flat, drunk as three sailors on shore leave. Make him strip in living room (very clever - will see why later), with Bernard playing proper butler, folding clothes like they're made of gold. His hands moving careful, practiced, like he done this many times before.

Take Lord to bedroom for special Kazakh rodeo show - he loving it like fat child love cake! When finished, he shower (second shower of night - first one was different kind, if you know what I mean), Bernard help dress him, very professional, very smooth, like he orchestrating dance he know by heart. Lord leaves £500 and - oh look! - American Express card fall from pocket by accident. What shame! Bernard say we keep safe for him, little smile playing on lips. Ha!

Next part of plan more complicated. Call Mfanni, invite her and Vertigo to Flying Tishkan restaurant to make peace. Make sure Bernard there, plus Arsen the Fake Kazakh (who now friend, sort of - in London, even fake Kazakh better than no Kazakh) has big men ready in case Vertigo tries gangster moves.

Big meeting at Flying Tishkan come next. Me and Bernard arrive late (on purpose, like rich people do), watch Mfanni and Vertigo go in first.

Inside, everything set up nice - Arsen playing perfect host, like he learn hospitality from YouTube video.

When we sit down, me and Mfanni share look - still remember good times, inventing special massage that make men cry (from happiness and wallet pain). But Vertigo, stupid man, start shouting about "scissor sisters" and "clams" like he learn English from toilet wall.

Feed them special goat meat (Jamaicans like goat, yes?), plus extra strong kumis that Arsen keep bringing. Soon they drunk like Russian tourists in Dubai. Bernard giving me secret winks whole time, like James Bond with eye problem.

Later, when Vertigo offers drive home, I say no - smart girl from Zanorkagon know better than get in pimp-mobile when plan in motion! We follow in Uber instead, watch police stop Vertigo's car. Very entertaining! Like reality TV show, but better because real and I wrote script! When we watch police put handcuffs on Vertigo, I feel happy like village girl who find out she not have to marry old man with no teeth.

Is funny thing about London - sometimes biggest gangster can be brought down by smallest butler with mobile phone. This city teaching me many things: how to survive, how to scheme, and most important - never trust pigeon or pimp. They both shit on you when you not looking.

CHAPTER 27

Rear View Mirror

Next morning, I give Bernard his orders. "Go shopping for food and house things!" He loves when I boss him - makes him feel important, like fancy butler in those BBC shows! When he comes back, I tell him, "Now clean apartment wearing only apron!" He gets excited while I sit like Queen Elizabeth (may she rest in peace) on my throne-chair, laughing at his pale English bottom wiggling in air.

Sometimes I sneak behind with feather duster, give little tickle to his man-bits when he bends for cleaning. Is my way of showing appreciation, yes? He accepts this payment like good English gentleman accepts tea - with stiff upper "lip"!

While Bernard shops at Harrods Bargain Supermarket, I sit alone with thoughts. Mind wanders to Zhanakorgan - my home, my family, someone else I cannot name, our animals, village life... and him. No, cannot say his name. Like London weather, some things better left not discussed.

I go to shower, catch sight in mirror. My legs and bottom still have marks. Bastard Mr. Smith's kamcha marks fade, but old scars from home? They stay faithful, like British to their terrible cooking. Then I see face.

Different scars there too. Others cannot see, but for me, always there, like smell of curry on Oxford Street.

Mirror is worse than London CCTV - always watching! In reflection, I don't see bathroom. I see past - faces of people left behind, all sad and scared like tourists who discover real price of London coffee. My mother, father, clown brother (very famous in three villages!), neighbors, and... him. Cannot look in his eyes. Only one smiling is evil one who marked me. He laughs at me through mirror "Look what your bad attitude did to everyone!"

I jump in shower, scrub with floor brush and kitchen pad like trying to clean London pigeon shit from statue in Trafalgar Square.

Painful? Yes. Bleeding? Little bit. But feel cleaner than Thames River (which is not saying much).

Bernard returns, and I check shopping. Notice how he buy exactly what needed without asking - like he read my mind, or maybe just know my habits too well. Give him new big list:

"Clean apartment! Make tidy! Prepare for evening work! Tonight, bring me Fisting Man!" Bernard nods like those bobbing dog toys in car windows,

"Certainly, Lapshagul. He will be yours."

He changes into cleaning costume - just apron, like sexy calendar but much more disturbing and scrubs floor on knees, his performance perfect. My job easier - use feather duster on his hanging bits until they shine brighter than Big Ben at night (which is also not saying much - London very dark city).

After two hours, coffee break. Bernard makes coffee perfect - exactly how I like, even tricks I never tell him. I sit on white sofa and Bernard sits on floor by feet, still in tiny apron, his man-parts looking sad like British summer. Disgusting! But need his brain thoughts - clever thoughts hiding behind pervert mask.

"What you think of me, how am I doing?" I ask. He says, "You're doing great. Soon you'll be queen of town." Words nice like London tourist brochure but face blank like window of closed betting shop.

Bernard puts on proper clothes, goes out for business. Alone again with crazy brain - more twisted than London street map! Try watching TV for distraction. But news comes on, and what do I see? Story about Vertigo and Mfanni, arrested with stolen things from Lord of U and K! There they are, being dragged to jail like Russian oligarch who forgot to pay bribe!!

I sit; mouth open wider than gap in London Underground doors. This what I want? Not sure. Maybe Bernard goes too far, like London rent prices. But I understand what happens, yes? Clear as London fog! Lord appears on screen, nervous and sweaty forehead, saying, "No idea when I lose American Express card." Ha! Of course, he not say truth! He won't announce, "Lost card while getting special shower from exotic lady!" No chance, like finding affordable flat in Zone 1!

Change channel fast! New story about government sending illegal immigrants to live on oil tanker in North Sea. My face turns green like moldy cheese in Tesco. Could never survive on boat - would die faster than houseplant in British winter. Only two weeks left on visa. Clock ticking louder than Big Ben!

Ding! Message from Bernard: "Have captured the Fister. Bringing now." Good! Can continue clever plan. Need many clever plans these days.

Have big money pile, yes, but also big trouble pile. Running fast just to stay still, like hamster in wheel at Pets at Home.

Soon Bernard brings special delivery: The Right Honourable Tarquin Fister, Minister of Immigration Services. Such fancy title! Even great Khans back home would say "Bloody hell, bit much!"

"Lappy Shaggy Girlie!" Fister shouts, drunk like Englishman on Friday night. "I've come for my Golden Shower of Steppe! Your

Bernard is very persistent and convincing!"

Think to self: Must do this again? Like bad London weather, answer is yes! If clever plan fails, will end up on North Sea boat or back in Zhanakorgan, where family will treat me worse than London treats vegetables. No choice! Must win.

While waiting for Minister Fister, I drink many weak English beers - making love in canoe, as Bernard says: "Fucking close to water!" My bladder now full, scared to move, might leak like British government secrets! So I tell Fister, "Tonight, special treat - Golden Shower of Steppe from standing position, a proud warrior queen!

Fister squeals like pig finding truffle: "Eeeeeaaah! Oooooh! Yessss!" More excited than Brit finding last Yorkshire pudding at Sunday roast! I stand over his belly - too many fish and chips - and let nature take course.

Not Golden Shower this time - more like Niagara Falls from Pink Cave of Wonders! Fister so happy, he makes own fountain faster than Boris Johnson changing political opinions. Right on Bernard's clean floor too - typical politician, making mess for others to clean!

After, Fister leaves tip big enough to buy small flat in Zone 6 (which is not saying much). But when he tries leaving, I stop him. "Mr. Minister Man," I say sweet like PG Tips with four sugars, "My visitor visa expiring very soon and I don't want to go. What you think about your Lappy need to leave?"

His face goes white. Starts stammering like Hugh Grant in every movie: "Er... how can I... beneath my pay grade... I... er..." I smile prettier than Kate Middleton at charity event. "Let me help your thinking, Minister," I say. "You make me special case, because we are special friends. You have special needs, yes? Needs that Daily Mail would love to hear about?"

He stands at door, stupid like tourist trying to make guard at

Buckingham Palace laugh. I continue: "I stay your special friend if I stay in U and K. But if I forced to leave? Maybe I become like WikiLeaks, you understand, yes?"

Message hits harder than London rain in winter. He nod like crazy puppet man, then run away fast. Bernard come out, watching Minister, grinning like cat who find exactly what he looking for. 'Think he understood,' he say, voice soft but satisfied. I make agreement noise, pretending not to notice how perfectly everything fall into place.

"Now, Bernard," I tell him, "Clean Minister's happy-time mess from floor. Keep evidence in fridge." Bernard agrees with that quick efficiency that sometimes make me wonder - he collecting these secrets like magpie collect shiny things, each piece fitting into puzzle I cannot see.

Life here like riding Boris bike through traffic - dangerous, expensive, but somehow still better than walking. Every day I learn more about surviving in this crazy city. Back home, biggest worry was if goats eat neighbor's washing. Here, worry about visa extensions, blackmail evidence, and whether Bernard remember to buy good toilet paper from Waitrose, not cheap stuff from Lidl that feel like sandpaper on tender parts.

But maybe I getting too good at London games. Starting to think like them - always planning, always watching back mirror like black cab driver. Is this progress or problem? Don't know. For now, just keep head above water in Thames of life, trying not to swallow too much.

CHAPTER 28

A Knock on the Door

Ha! You know something funny? I love this crazy life!

Yesterday I was doing big complaining, like old babushka with bad back, about always having to watch front and back same time. But truth is hitting me like slap from angry mama: I'm getting kick from this!

This game we play, tiger and rat game (I am tiger, obviously - have you seen my magnificent mustache?), it makes me feel alive like disco night in Almaty. I swat away annoying rats trying to bite my behind, while living fancy London life with champagne and caviar - though caviar here is garbage compared to proper Kazakh stuff, if you want my honest opinion. Sometimes I dream: one day I go home big hero, yes? Build school, hospital, maybe even indoor toilet for whole village! Everyone say "Look at our girl who went to London and came back golden!" And then - BOOM! - knock on door interrupts my beautiful dream.

Bernard is not home to answer, so I walk to door slow-slow, like approaching angry bear. No need for spy hole - nose already tells me who stands there, stinking up my nice hallway with his police smell. I open door and - SURPRISE! - there stands Dick Clitter, trying to look like fancy TV detective but looking more like wet dog in borrowed clothes.

His tie is hanging, and his raincoat probably hasn't seen dry cleaner since Queen Elizabeth was girl.

"Well, hello Constable Clitter! They finally trust you with big-boy clothes, yes?" I say with smile that probably looks like constipated camel. He pushes past me, hands still in pockets like they're glued there. Maybe they are? English people very strange about touching things.

I follow him to living room, trying to be good host like mama taught me: "In my country, we take shoes off, wipe feet, show respect for-"

"Sweetheart," he cuts me off, voice soft like snake in grass, "let's be clear about something. This isn't your village anymore. This is London. my London."

I stand there, mouth open like fish at market. Then he adds one more word that makes my stomach do flip-flop: "Yet."

Oh blyat. Now I'm thinking maybe I should have stayed home and married cousin Azamat's goat like mama suggested in one her nicer rants. My mouth goes dry, and when I speak, voice comes out squeaky like mouse at cat convention...

"What you mean?" I squeak.

"You know exactly what I mean," says Clitter, face still wearing smug smile. "And I bet you know how I found your little nest here, don't you?"

Words stick in my throat like stale bread. I just stand there, praying to all gods of steppe that Bernard will appear like magic genie.

Clitter makes himself comfortable on my sofa - very rude, didn't even ask! - crosses legs and lights cigarette like he owns place. Blows smoke everywhere.

"Had an interesting chat today," he says, "with Lord Blithering. Lost his American Express card few days ago. Says maybe he left it here, in this..." - looks around my room like he inspecting goat pen - "...charming residence. What you reckon about that, Lappy Shag? His lordship been paying you little visits, has he?

And what exactly you two been up to, eh?"

"And what fucking business is that of yours, PC Clitter?"

Then - like he been waiting for perfect moment - Bernard appears! Not rushing, not dramatic, just sliding into scene like actor who know exactly when to make entrance. I stay quiet, watching Clitter look up at Bernard who now looms over him like angry mountain, face arranged in perfect mask of outrage.

"Still waiting for an answer, officer. What gives you right to barge in here without a warrant, asking questions like the KGB?"

Then Bernard starts shouting - ai-yi-yi, such language! Would make even taxi driver in Astana blush! All about going to Police Chief, making complaints, throwing words around like "harassment" and "abuse of power."

"You wanted Vertigo, she got him gift-wrapped for you. Plus, his criminal girlfriend! What more you do want – a golden ticket to a chocolate factory?"

Clitter sits there, silent like frozen fish. His brain working overtime - can almost see smoke coming from ears. Bernard has him pinned like butterfly in display case.

I decide maybe is time to play good cop (ha! is funny because he is bad cop, yes?). "Dear Officer Clitter," I say in voice smooth like expensive vodka, "you got what you wanted from me. So maybe now we forget about other things?" I smile nicey-nicey, like when trying to convince border guard that suspicious package is just traditional Kazakh cheese.

Clitter gets up slow-slow, heads for door, but turns at last moment like bad guy in movie: "If Lord Blithering makes official complaint about... activities... in this flat, I come back for you, Lapshaggy. Bank on it!"

After door slams, I turn to look at Bernard, with question in eyes.

"Don't worry about that police puppy," he says, "His lordship is never going to stand in court explaining what happened here."

I'm thinking here comes part where Bernard wants payment for helping. Like clockwork, yes? Wait for it... wait for it...

"Oh darling," he purrs like cat in heat, but something about way he ask for favors always so... calculated. Like he know exactly when to play pervert card. "I have this terrible itch that needs scratching..." Then - bozhe moy! - down go trousers like stock market crash.

"Sacred ancestors!" I sigh. "Is impossible for you to do any favor without wanting sexy payment?"

He wiggles bottom like belly dancer. "Ooh yes, scold me more! I've been very naughty boy!" Sometimes I wonder if his need for punishment real, or if each humiliation just another move in game I not understand. But body want what body want, so I get special tickle-whip from secret drawer (very good quality, brought from home - London ones break too easy), and give Bernard his "reward." Whippy-stroke here, whippy-stroke there, like conductor leading orchestra of pain and pleasure.

Someday I think maybe I should write book - "How to Succeed in London Without Really Trying (But With Lots of Whipping)" by Lappy Shag. Would be bestseller, no?

CHAPTER 29

My Idea of Fun

S o, is it?

'Is what?' you are probably asking right now.

Is life fun, I keep asking myself like broken record in village disco - am I really, really enjoying this crazy circus?

Yes, yes, I'm loving power and winning and pulling sneaky tricks like expert puppet master, but is this actually what smart person calls 'fun'?

Or maybe it's just making tingles in my belly and my special lady parts because my ego is getting fat like prize-winning cow at father's village festival - all show, no good for actual riding.

I'm thinking these deep thoughts while soaking in fancy bath that costs more than whole year of village wages, and Bernard is cleaning apartment dressed in what looks like black garbage bag made into human costume, with red ball stuck in mouth like apple in roasted pig. Stupid pervert man can barely breathe - serves him right!

Ya Allah, if babushka could see me now, living with rubber-wearing weirdo and making rich men pay good money to... well, let's just say not for English lessons!

I slide under bubbles, holding breath until lungs scream. When I pop up like cork from expensive champagne bottle, I have revelation hit me harder than Uncle Nurlan's homebrewed vodka.

Next thing, I'm getting out of bath, trying to dry off while

Bernard follows me around in leather costume, making weird noises with his... actually, better not to tell what he's doing. I'm naked as day I was born, searching for clothes that won't make me look like walking advertisement for sinful lifestyle, and he keeps getting in way. 'Fuck off, Bernard!' I shout, 'Go guard flat from burglars!' He agrees like good little pet. (What costume he'll wear for guard duty, I don't want to know - probably dress up as Queen's Guard but with much less cloth involved).

I put on my normal person disguise: jeans with strategical placed holes, boring shirt, leather jacket that screams 'I ride motorcycle' (I don't), and boots big enough for village giant. Mirror shows me different girl - not Lapshagul the Whip-Master, but just Lapshagul who maybe could walk down street without making people's eyebrows jump up like scared rabbits.

But who am I kidding? One normal outfit doesn't wash away things I do for living. Like they say in London - you can take girl out of weird sex parties, but... actually, nobody says that here. Is just sad truth.

I escape flat (and Bernard's rubber squeaking) into street – the area reminds me of home, if home was even more broken and had more angry people with knife collection hobbies. My fancy apartment is like putting diamond ring on pig's nose - looks expensive but still smells like pig.

Should be living in Knightsbridge or BelgraviaPoshPants where other rich people live, but having bank account fat like American tourist doesn't make you classy when you spend days doing things that would make priest faint and nights looking over shoulder for trouble.

My boots clump-clump-clump on broken pavement as if mind of their own. Fine, stupid boots, take me where you want - I trust you more than I trust my own judgment lately. But then...

'Blyad! Not here, you traitor boots!' I say out loud when I see where feet have brought me. My head spins but is not from drink or drugs - is pure crazy living in my brain now! Standing at door of Zig Zag Club like moth to very hot flame. And you know what worst part is? I'm going in. Why? Because this - this crazy, dangerous, probably very stupid decision - this is what I call fun now!

Walk downstair, heart doing traditional folk dance in chest. Looking for trouble because trouble is only friend who never stands me up. Then I see her - sitting alone like spider waiting for fly, wearing black dress that shows more skin than village wedding fight. Her chest trying to escape dress and that smile painted on red lips. Is smile that says 'Come closer, I have candy' - but candy probably poisoned.

In this moment, truth hits me like slap from angry babushka: tonight will be night when trouble and freedom make sexy dance together. And yes, I am ready! Finally, like seeing through vodka-clear water, I understand what was missing in my life back in glorious Kazakhstan (besides working toilets).

All fancy London things - sparkly dresses that cost more than village virgin, shopping in stores where people look at you like you might steal diamond-covered toilet brush - these things were not filling hole in my heart. Being Kazakh Queen of London Town? Pfft. What I wanted was to be free like eagle soaring over steppe! (But with better fashion sense, obviously.)

Mfanni seems me and fixes her eyes on me like a snake ready to strike. When I see Mfanni's evil smile spread like poison, I don't even flinch. My hands go in pockets, casual-casual, like I learned from watching British gangster movies.

"Hello Mfanni," I say, walking toward her like brave woman who definitely not scared of getting punched in face. "Hello Lappy," she says back, nastiness melting from her lips like snow in spring. Then - SURPRISE! - she hugs me like wrestling champion bear from Kirghiz circus. My hands are trapped in pants, making me look like confused penguin trying to dance. When she finally let go, I can breathe again and say, "I come to make peace..."

"What?! Fuck off!" she barks. "Last time we made 'peace,' I spent 24 hours in a cell that smelled worse conch left rotting in the Kingston sun! What trick you planning now?"

Her face does strange dance between smile and snarl - in London, I learn this means either person is joking or about to stab you. Very confusing!

"You were col-lat-eral damage," I say, proud of using fancy English word I learned from action movies. "Trick was meant for Vertigo. Not our fault you go home with him like lovesick donkey."

She thinks about this, nodding head. "Yeah, suppose you're right," she says. "Let's drink!"

Few minutes later, we sit at table like old times, when I was fresh off boat (actually was plane, but boat sounds more dramatic) and she teach me tricks of London underground. Not actual underground - though that also very confusing with all colored lines - but criminal underground.

Much more exciting!

"Where is Vertigo?" I ask. She shrugs brown shoulders like throwing off annoying thought. "In the boob," she says. I look confused - many English words still mystery to me, like why they call sausages 'bangers' when they make no bang. She explains: "Prison. Jail. The big house."

Ah! Like gulag but with better food! She tells me Vertigo took blame for credit card thing, so now she run Zig Zag club while he sits in fancy English prison.

Am I worried about sitting in criminal club with girlfriend of jailed gangster? Ha! This is nothing! Back home, women's book club more dangerous - last meeting, three casualties over argument about romance novel ending.

But then, like curse from angry ancestor, who should appear? Same Albanians from before - the ones who caused big trouble with Vertigo! You remember, yes? The ones who made even tough Mfanni nervous. Three men built like brick outhouses (another strange English saying - why would house for toilet need to be strong?), faces mean as hungry wolves. They take drinks without paying, tell pretty hostess girls to go away with words that would make even my Uncle Boris blush.

I recognize their leader right away - same face scar, same silver teeth that probably cost more than my father's best horse. Last time we met...how you say...things got complicated. Now here they are again like bad weather that follows you home.

When Mfanni tries to show brave face, they laugh at her like hyenas. "They think I'm trannie!" she tells me, fury in eyes. "Can't believe woman runs club!"

That's when I feel it - special anger that comes from depths of Kazakh soul. I reach for my kamcha. One quick snap - WHOOSH! - and leader's eyeball pop out like champagne cork! He screams, and other two run away faster than my cousin Borush when he see tax collector.

Mfanni not happy though. "They come back with army!" she panic. But I just smile mysterious smile of steppe warrior (I practice this in mirror). I have plan. Maybe crazy plan, but in London, I learn that crazy plans sometimes work best. Besides, what worst can happen? (Note to self: maybe stop asking this question - universe likes to answer it too much.)

CHAPTER 30

Showtime!

H a! So there we are, me and Mfanni, sitting pretty with fancy Western cocktails (mine tastes like grandmother's cough syrup). Mfanni, poor thing, she freaks out. Me? I'm cool like cucumber in snow, watching door like hawk watches mouse. Because in London club, you must always watch door - this I learn quick!

BOOM! Like avalanche in Tian Shan mountains, down comes Alboscum gang. Seven angry men, all looking like they eat nails for breakfast and wash down with battery acid. "Where is whip-bitch?" they shout, which is not very nice way to address lady, even one who sometimes hit people with traditional Kazakh weapon.

They thought they were hunting me. But funny thing about hunting—you don't realize when you're the one being led into the trap. We hide in shadow, but London clubs have too many bright lights - not like good proper yurt where shadows are proper shadows! Big mistake - one sees me. His eyes get small like angry weasel, and he pushes through crowd. "You! Snake woman!" he shouts. (At least this better than previous name, yes?)

I jump on stage where ladies usually dance with not many clothes (in London, this is culture, they tell me). Music starts - not good traditional dombra music, but boom-boom noise that makes ears hurt. But when in London nightclub, dance like Londoner, yes? So, I move like having seizure, which seems to be correct style here.

Uh oh! Mr. Angry pulls out gun - and not ceremonial type like back home! Real bang-bang gun! I flick kamcha. He dodge once, twice- this one clearly not first time in whip fight. Other Alboscum yelling bad words - some I know from English class, others I must look up later in Google.

Then - SNAP! - my kamcha finds target! His neck sprays red like festival fountain, but less festive, more messy. Rest look surprised - clearly, they not expect traditional Kazakh herding tool to be so effective urban weapon!

Poor Mfanni tries to be hero, grabs fallen gun like she sees in American movies. Bad idea! In my country, we learn to ride horse age three, use whip age five, but nobody teach us proper London gunfight! BANG! She goes down screaming - so dramatic, this girl!

Finally, police arrive - late as always, like second-hand camel to racing derby. Newly promoted Chief Inspector Clitter bursts in with team, all shouting fancy police words, numbers. Everything goes crazy - guns, shouting, breaking glass. Just like home during wedding party, except here nobody dancing and having fun!

I finally escape in ambulance with Mfanni (free ride across London - very smart, yes?), leaving Clitter to clean mess. He always blame me anyway!

Later, watching city lights from hospital window, I think: Kazakh life simple - tend animals, respect elders, don't make trouble. London life complicated - dodge bullets, outsmart gangsters, try not to get deported. But exciting! Like reality TV show, but you might die! Still... maybe next time I try nice quiet English pub instead. I hear they only fight with fists there, like civilized people.

CHAPTER 31

The Morning After the Night Before

Here I am, stuck in hospital like forgotten potato in back of cupboard. Nine hours! Nine! Same time it takes to fly from Almaty to London, but at least on plane they give you food and blanket. Here? Just plastic chair trying to murder my ass and lights so bright they make morgue look cozy.

They won't let me see Mfanni. "Big surgery," they say, like I don't know what bullet in belly means. Oh Mfanni, my poor friend! First I get you locked up with police like common street criminal, now I get you shot like... well, like common street criminal again. Fire in my belly has turned to ice cube - actually, whole body feels like ice cube in freezer of depression.

Doctor comes, face serious like tax collector, tells me Mfanni still sleeping beauty from drugs they gave her. Says I should go home before I become patient too. For once, I listen to man in white coat.

Back at flat, Bernard waits like nervous chihuahua. He knows everything already - in London, news spreads like STD in university dormitory. "How is she?" he squeaks, then starts crying like baby who lost favorite toy. Says it's all his fault for working with Sheikh and getting mixed up in this tornado of violence.

Looking at Bernard's tiny legs and big head wobbling as he cries, I realize something: in London, it's always little men with big mouths who make biggest mess. Like watching pit of snakes trying to organize dinner party - lots of hissing, no progress.

To shut up his crying (and because my body feels like it got run over by herd of angry yak), I let Bernard give me bubble bath. He scrubs my back like good servant should, massages toes that have seen too much running. Then I put on my warrior outfit - ripped jeans, leather jacket, boots that could kick through wall. No more Harrods princess dress-up for me - I look like circus tent that got into fight with paint factory when I try fancy clothes anyway. Kazakh sun must have fried my fashion sense along with my brain.

At street market, shopping for tougher jacket (because clearly I need more leather), who appears like bad penny? CI-fucking Clitter. "Playing tough girl now?" he says in my face. I strike back fast like desert cobra:

"Have to be tough when police are soft like baby's bottom!"

But something strange happens. Instead of fight, I see man crack like egg dropped on floor. He tells me about his injured officers, voice shaking like leaf in wind. I see proud police peacock turn into sad pigeon, and instead of feeling good, I feel... bad? What is happening to me? Am I getting soft like runny cheese?

So I do most un-Kazakh thing possible - I hug him! Yes, wrap myself around this broken man like mother bear comforting cub. At first he's stiff as Soviet border guard, then melts in my arms.

Now we sit in pub called Black Cross (why English love such depressing names for drinking places?), drinking whiskey in dark corner (again with dark corners!). He tries to act tough again, apologizing for being "weak." Old me would have laughed, called him woman in man's uniform.

Instead, my mouth says wise things about everyone having soft spots, like philosopher who drinks too much.

When our eyes meet over whiskey glasses, I see something

that scares me more than angry Sheikh with gun - I see understanding. Oh God, am I becoming... civilized? Quick, someone bring me kumis before I turn completely English!

So, there we are, getting friendly with Mr. J. Daniels, three or four times over. Not talking much, just watching pub life like it's Discovery Channel special on British wildlife. The Black Cross is filling up with what I call London's finest specimens - the kind that make you wonder if Darwin got evolution backwards.

Clitter says I should leave because it's getting "dangerous." Ha! Like morning traffic in Almaty isn't dangerous. But then - святая корова! – in through door walk two Albogoons from last night's... let's call it "disagreement." I turn to Clitter, ready to kick his ass, but before I can open mouth, these two are walking toward us like wolves who spot injured lamb.

I feel Clitter shaking next to me, and I think, "Ah, so brave English police officer is actually scared rabbit." But no - I look at him and see he's not scared at all. He's... growing? Like those American muscle movies where green man ruins perfectly good shirt. Then Clitter does something that makes my brain stop working - he puts out hand to shake with lead Alboscum, like they're meeting for afternoon tea!

"Good to see you, Dickie," says gold-tooth wonder, who apparently goes by name of Ballsak. (No Kazakh mother would ever curse child with such name.)

And there I am, mouth opening and closing like fish at market wondering why it's not in water anymore. My bumhole is clenched tighter than camel's backside in sandstorm. Both men are grinning at me like I'm best joke they've heard all year.

I stand up, wobbly, and tell Clitter exactly what I think: "You have head of shit, and you used me."

Clitter laughs like child who knows where cookie is hidden. "What are you on about, Lappy? This is London - everything goes round and round, cuts both ways."

I think London is not carousel, and I am not wooden horse going up and down, round and round. As Uncle Boltok would say after third bottle,"tipti dauissinis silkinip ketkende day aqiqating aitiniz" - even when voice shakes like leaf in wind, speak your truth.

So I scream at him again, hand wrapped around kamcha in pocket like it's security blanket made of leather and pain.

Then Ballsak - this golden-toothed blessing to dental industry - tells me I did him favor by... how you say... "removing" his cousin last night.

Apparently, in London, family feuds are solved by outsourcing to confused Kazakh girls with anger management issues.

"You see?" Clitter says, "There are two sides to everything. Stop playing holy virgin - we all know what you do for living."

I sit down but keep hand on kamcha. In Kazakhstan, we trust Allah. In London, I trust leather whip in pocket.

So now I learn truth. I'm murderer (promotion from club hostess!), friends with corrupt cop who probably couldn't find crime if it danced naked in front of him wearing Christmas lights, and Albanian gangster who thinks family reunions are best held in morgue.

So much for my dream of being Kazakh Princess of London, shopping at Harrods, wearing pink pearls! No, I'm now Kazakh assassin - like James Bond, but with better cheekbones and worse English. And instead of fancy car and martini, I get drunk cop and Albanian mafia as new best friends.

I leave Black Cross without word, leaving Clitter to drink with his cockroach friends. Back home, we say: better to walk alone in desert than share saddle with scorpions. In London, I learn:

sometimes scorpions wear police badges and give you thumbs up for murder.

CHAPTER 32

Turning the Tide

I am sitting in apartment with Bernard, trying to have serious talk like grown-up person. This is proving difficult because this complete moron is dressed as giant mouse.

Not small mouse - we are talking full furry costume with whiskers that look like they were stolen from street sweeper's broom, and ears big enough to catch satellite TV from Moscow.

Through his fake teeth (which look like they belong to British beaver), he is making squeaky demands for pussy to feed him cheese. I try not to laugh because I am angry, so I say with straight face, "Which pussy you are meaning exactly, Bernard?" Then he does mouse giggle that sounds like pig having asthma attack, and his fake whiskers are dancing like drunk uncle at wedding.

My life! One day I am accidentally making men dead, next day I join crime family like it is job application at Tesco, now I am feeding dairy products to grown man in mouse costume - from place that mother told me was only for making babies and peeing! What would babushka think if she saw me now? In bathroom mirror, I stare at self while cleaning cheese crumbs from... how you say... lady garden. I am thinking I must escape this crazy situation, but this will be like trying to push cow through cat door - backwards!

Then Bernard is normal again (well, normal for Bernard), telling me, "Tonight you have special guest - Minister Fister!" First I am confused, then brain catches up - ah yes, immigration man. "Wow Bernard," I say, trying to sound impressed but feeling like chicken who just notice chef sharpening knife, "he must really like our hospitality, yes?"

Bernard's face gets that smile - you know, the one that says, 'I just farted in elevator but will blame old lady.' He says, "I made him an offer in the gentleman's club. One he cannot refuse."

My stomach is doing more gymnastics. How much trouble can one Kazakh girl handle in two days? I am already burning up like overworked towel boy in sauna! "What kind of offer?" I ask. His answer makes me want to throw up borscht I ate three weeks ago, so I run from flat into London air.

Outside is cold like Siberian toilet seat, wind trying to slap sense into me through leather jacket. My ripped jeans (which cost more than my village's monthly potato budget) are useless against cold. In my head, thoughts are screaming. Am I angry? Scared? Both?

Everyone here is either pervert or criminal - sometimes at same time! And me? I came here innocent girl fresh from Zhanakorgan, now I am turning into killing machine who does sex work! What in name of holy horse balls is happening?!

I find bench in small park, away from cars that try to kill you while pretending to be polite about it. I sit, arms crossed thinking about what life would be if I stayed home. Ha! Easy answer - I would be dead. Yes, maybe now I work like crazy yak, but back home I was like three-legged goat with depression. But this yak phase? Temporary! Soon I will transform - from tired farm animal into mighty snow leopard! At least... this is what I tell self while eating cheese crumbs from purse.

Suddenly, feeling someone sit next to me. Keep eyes closed because in London, opening eyes often leads to regret. "Thought I find you here," says Mfanni, voice quiet like mouse (normal mouse, not Bernard mouse). "How are you?" I ask, eyes still doing impression of Lenin statue.

"Okay," she says, "Police shut down club. Changed locks like landlord trying to collect rent money."

I ask if they can do this, and she tells me yes - serious crime means serious consequences. My laugh sounds like hyena with hiccups and say, "Vertigo will be more angry than bull who sat on cactus when he gets out." We both laugh, then go to Flying Tishkan for coffee, gossiping like old village witches planning curses on stupid men. Just another normal day in London for Kazakh girl!

So we're putting bozo in our coffee as if normal thing to do, and two hours later we're flying high like grandmother's bread in storm. Good times, yes?

Then I look at clock and remember - oh blyat! - I must return to fancy apartment for giving Golden Shower of Steppe to Minister Fister.

When I tell Mfanni this, she laughs so hard I think she might break something important inside her face. Her teeth are like lighthouse in dark sea of London smog. That's when brilliant idea hits me like loose brick from Soviet-era apartment.

I bring Mfanni back to my place - my beautiful slice of capitalist heaven. She's looking around. "Wowee!" she says, "Not bad for the girl who used to live in yurt!" She's touching my cream carpets with her eyes, stroking my white walls with her brain, getting too friendly with my fancy kitchen gadgets that I still don't know names for.

Then she asks about rent price, and I tell her to mind her own fucking business - in politest way possible, of course. That's when she shows true colors like snake shedding fake skin.

"But Lapshagul," she says, not laughing anymore, "I don't have a fucking business anymore, do I? Not like you." Her voice has more poison than bad mushroom soup from Uncle Nurlan's wedding.

Now I'm getting angry. "Listen here, you think I'm some common street walker? I am specialist massage therapist for very particular gentlemen. Very particular! Is art form!"

Just then, Bernard comes out from bathroom, blinking, and asking why I brought guest when Important Customer is coming. "Don't worry, Bernard," I say, "Mfanni is just leaving." And whoosh! - she's gone like wind through yurt flap, but with much more door slamming.

Oh dear. Oh deary dear dear. I'm thinking now I've made big mistake, Mfanni will be jealous like cat watching other cat eat premium tuna.

She'll blame me for everything - Vertigo in jail, Zig Zag club closed, while I'm living life of luxury with high-class clients and proper toilet that flushes every time. The chickens of karma are coming home to make nest in my hair, as we say in village.

Then-buzzzz goes door. Bernard answers intercom in his fancy butler voice that he practices in mirror: "Yes Minister, please come right up, sir." He sounds like Queen's personal tea pourer.

Twenty minutes later, I'm marching on Minister's buttocks like proud soldier in very strange parade. Hi-fi is blasting Kazakh State Orchestra while I'm giving special performance of national anthem, modified for occasion. Each squirt of golden rain matches music perfectly - I'm artist, you see? Professional!

'Golden rain from my nunu, (squirt)

Golden rain on your bum, (squirt)

A tale of brave deeds done, (squirt)

Behold homeland's rising sun! (squirt)

From this place in belly, known as my bladder (squirt)

My glory pour down like water, (squirt)

Never surrender your honour, (squirt)

My proud Kazakh daughter!' (squirt, squirt, squirt!)'

Minister is squealing like happy pig in mud bath, turning over so I can give chest same treatment. And then as he sees how patriotic my nunu is, all over faster than he can say 'God Save Queen.' Perhaps with vision in head of royal lady and his chance of a tap on the shoulder with a sword disappearing fast, he deflates like a punctured tire.

I skip to bathroom where Bernard waits with fluffy towel like good servant should. We stand there with serious faces in mirror-covered bathroom, waiting for Minister Fister to do walk of shame.

He shuffles in, trying to cover private parts like shy schoolboy. Perfect - we have him exactly where we want him, feeling naked as newborn in Siberian winter. When he asks for clothes (which Bernard has cleverly hidden), phone (also hidden), we play little game of "We need to talk business" until he finally understands situation. Like training stubborn donkey, sometimes you must repeat yourself many times.

Finally, he takes picture of my visa with shaking hands, then notices special video on his phone - one starring him in very compromising position, complete with my musical performance. His face goes white like belly of dead fish. "You bastards," he whispers, holding phone like it might bite him. I agree we are bastards.

"Minister," I say, "you are supposed to be intelligent man with important position but as we say back home, "Fool who teases snake must be ready to hop on one leg."

"Now, about my new visa..." He pays up and leaves faster than pickpocket at village festival."

Bernard is looking pleased with himself, wanting favors from his boss and worshipful mistress. His eyebrows doing little dance on his face. I tell him "Fuck off, I'm exhausted!" Then take nice cold shower and go to bed - has been very long day.

But sleep is playing hard to get. I'm tossing and turning; ceiling starts spinning and walls close in like hungry predators. When it finally comes, it's deep, like bottom of Caspian Sea - no dreams, just warm blackness. Is how I hope death will be, minus snoring.

Next morning, sun is shining through window, and Bernard brings English breakfast tea - one of few things about U and K that makes sense. For once, pervy little jerboa isn't trying to trick me into something weird. He's dressed like normal person instead of pervert drama queen, which makes me suspicious immediately. In my experience, when Bernard looks normal, universe is probably about to explode.

He suggests day off from what he calls 'piss and jizz factory' - I don't like name but is accurate like arrow hitting yak's backside. We go shopping, making strange pair in London streets - me in leather jacket like rebel cowgirl from steppe, him in checked suit like someone shrunk English gentleman in hot wash.

I'm whole hand taller than Bernard in my boots, and when I see our reflection in shop windows, I start giggling like teenage girl who just saw boy fall off horse on head. But then I notice something strange - other people not laughing. Maybe in London, tall woman with tiny man in silly hat is normal thing. This city is crazy like that.

Bernard takes me everywhere in London, walking more than nomad searching for lost camel. But I start noticing something sneaky - everywhere we go, he knows people. He's saying hello in voice loud enough to wake dead ancestors, showing me off like prize. Normally, this would make me angry, but today I'm thinking - if little Bernard wants to parade me around as trophy, why not? Could be worse - could be peeing on other minister.

We end up in Soho bistro - fancy name for place that serves food on plates size of my palm. Then Bernard takes me to pub full of people just like him - all a bit strange, like flock of sheep where every sheep thinks it's not a sheep. These people don't fit in normal world. And suddenly I'm feeling warm inside, like after good bowl of kumis. Maybe this is what English people call happiness, though probably they call it something more complicated with extra syllables.

Evening comes, and I say we should go back to flat - customers will be waiting for special treatments. But Bernard makes excuse about visiting mother in north London. When he leaves, he looks back at me through window with sad eyes. He waves goodbye, and something in my stomach feels wrong. I'm holding kamcha handle tighter and tighter in pocket, thinking maybe trouble is coming like avalanche in mountains.

This feeling gets worse with each whiskey I drink. Bernard never visits mother - she died three years ago from eating bad fish pie, he told me this many times when drunk. Something is very wrong. But what can I do? I'm sitting here in pub full of London weirdos, drinking whiskey that costs more than month's rent back home, while life is probably falling apart like cheap Chinese motorcycle.

Is funny thing about London - just when you think you understand this crazy city, it shows you new way to make your life complicated. But what can you do? In Zhanakorgan, we have saying: "When riding wild horse, better to hold on than worry about where it's going." So I order another round and hold on tight to my kamcha. Whatever's coming, at least I'm not giving golden showers tonight.

And maybe that's real victory in this crazy city - sometimes best thing is just to sit in pub, drink overpriced whiskey, and wait for storm to pass. Though in my experience, storm usually just bringing bigger storm, like matryoshka dolls of trouble.

Is taking forever to walk back to Elephants Castle, too many big English whiskeys making my brain swim like confused sturgeon. I do special drunk dance all way home: one step forward like brave soldier, one step sideways like circus clown, one step back like scared rabbit, repeat repeat repeat for many hours. Finally arrive at door-but what this? Key not going in lock Like trying to put camel through eye of needle, as my grandmother say (she was very wise woman, but also little bit crazy).

Then - BOOM! - door opens by itself like magic trick, except no magic, just Ballsak standing there with smug hyena face! You remember Ballsak, yes? Clitter's Albanian friend from Black Cross pub, always smelling of cheap aftershave and bad intentions.

I try make quick move with my kamcha, but my hands right now are like noodles in a bowl of kespe. Ballsak catch it too easy, then WHOOSH! - I go flying through door like bag of potatoes thrown by angry market woman. Inside apartment (my apartment!), I see whole circus of disaster: one Albo wearing Bernard's mouse costume and dancing like fool, another one making my beautiful white sofa dirty with his boots and kebab grease. High class!

"Welcome home, Lappy!" Ballsak say with voice honey covered in broken glass. "Oh wait, is not your home anymore - but don't worry, you still have job here!" They laugh like pack of jackals they are.

Is then I realize terrible thing, like black sun rising in morning of hell - I have been betrayed worse than Caesar (who at least only got stabbed once). Clitter, Mfanni, even Bernard ('Et tu, Bernardo?' as dead Roman would say), they all sold me like cheap goat at market.

This story getting darker than bottom of well at midnight, but what can I do? Sometimes in life, you think you smart fox, but turn out you actually stupid chicken in fox's dinner plan.

I try standing up but legs not working like puppet with cut strings, and stomach doing bad gymnastics routine. Then Ballsak grab my arm and push me into chair. He tower over me like Gadzilya "Now, Lappy Shaggy Gully, let me explain new our new business arrangement."

I try find words to tell how I feel, but even my special Borat-style talking not enough anymore. In my homeland language, I could tell you pain like thousand angry scorpions in heart, but English words too slippery like wet fish. Maybe I just say: I wish I was dead like uncle Boltabek's favorite dog (who ate poisonous mushrooms and exploded - very sad day in village).

Ballsak lean close to my face, breath stinking like raki. "From now, you stay here, we will take care of everything. No need for you to leave apartment, we bring food, drinks, make you a very happy relaxed worker bee, yes?" While he talking, I collecting special surprise in mouth - mixture of spit and hate, very traditional in homeland for showing respect to enemies. Then - PTHHH! - I shoot this gift straight into his eye like champion camel in spitting contest!

"Dirty animal!" he screaming, "Now you learn lesson!" But before revenge party can start, someone grab my hair from behind, pulling like they trying to start old Soviet tractor. I kick at Ballsak but he use my own kamcha against me - very disrespectful to whip's cultural heritage!

Pain is like fire ants having picnic on my legs, but I not screaming. Instead, I use voice like desert demon possessed by bigger desert demon: "Kill me now, or you die screaming later." I say this many times, slow like honey dripping from dead bee's bottom, even while legs feeling like they visited angry butcher.

Someone holding my shoulders down, breath smelling like he eat garbage for breakfast, lunch, AND dinner. In middle of pain, I having strange thought about why all Albanians not knowing about toothbrush - maybe is too expensive in their country? But then everything go black.

When I wake up, situation has gone from bad kebab to terrible kebab with extra wrong sauce. I naked as baby (but less crying, more drugs), tied to bed like part of religious sacrifice. Everything feeling fuzzy and warm, swimming in cloud made of wool. Even rope on wrists feeling friendly, which definitely not normal - in homeland, rope never your friend unless professional hangman.

Feel like floating in warm milk bath, thinking soft thoughts like baby's bottom. These Albanian devils have filled me with more drugs than medicine woman's special winter tea! Is strange because last time I was tied up like this (long story involving angry husband and missing vodka), I was not feeling so... nice? Drugs making everything seem okay, which making me more angry, except I too relaxed to be proper angry. Is like trying to be fierce wolf but actually being sleepy puppy.

Then voice come like bad radio: "Drink! Suck!" and plastic tube appear in mouth. I try dodge it like avoiding village zhaushy but body too weak. So I drink, because what choice I have? Is only water, but Ballsak watching me like hawk eyeing very drunk mouse. He says need full bladder - high class entertainment coming soon, I think with brain full of cotton wool and sadness.

Water filling me up like balloon at children's party, except this party definitely not for children. When I full as festival wineskin, Ballsak take away tube and tell me, "No peeing in bed, or kamcha will sing special song on your skin!"

Then everything become dream you have after eating moldy bread. Men coming and going, me getting untied for special performance (like circus bear, except bear have more dignity), and out of eye corner, Albanian counting money quicker than my grandmother could count sheep - and she was champion sheep counter in three villages!

Later (maybe hours, maybe days), I back on bed, hands tied again. Feel needle in arm like mosquito who went to medical school. I not looking because sometimes in life, like when mother-in-law cooking experimental meal, is better not to see what happening.

Death feeling is very friendly now, like warm blanket on cold day. Why everyone so scared of death? Is like being worried about going to sleep, except less farting and more forever. Everything floating nice, riding cloud made of dreams, looking down at my life like watching movie with very bad actress playing main part. Nobody angry, nobody blame, just warm white velvet everywhere.

But then - KABOOM! - everything explode! World become crazy circus of yellow and blue lights and shouting and hands everywhere. I see Ballsak going down slower than grandmother's dumpling in throat, police stick making special music with his head. Other Albos on floor crying like babies who lose favorite toy. These police not normal London bobby- bobby with funny hat- these ones mean business.

And who leading this party? Of course! Like bad penny always turning up. Detective Superofficer Dick "Fuckwit" Clitter!

He put face close to mine, breathing important police breath: "What I tell you Lappy? What goes around comes around. Like the Ouroboros!"

I thinking maybe drugs making me stupid, but even sober person with PhD in philosophy not understand this crazy talk. But Clitter smile like cat who not just eat canary but also sell canary's cage for profit. And even with brain swimming in drug soup, I realize something very important - this man I call fuckwit and worse things (many worse things, some not translatable to English) is now saving my life like hero in bad movie.

Then everything become ambulance lights and hospital beeping. I must have gone to sleep, because next thing I know, I wake up in hospital bed. This is logic, yes? Like saying water is wet or politician is liar - must sleep before wake.

I open eyes and see past forest of medical tubes and wires to face of Dickie Boy. Of course he here - who else? In normal story, hero is brave policeman who work for glorious government. But maybe this not normal story! Maybe this modern story with more twists than pretzel maker with hiccups!

"The gluttonous snake eat its own tail," Clitter say, again with the fortune cookie philosophy. I think: yes, sure, snake eats tail, then eats body, then eats own face and - POOF! - disappear like magic trick! Just like truth in London - everyone going round and round eating own lies until nothing left except big pile of trouble with fancy English accent.

"How are you feeling?" he ask, as if we friends who meet for tea and crumpets. "Fine," I say, not wanting conversation with this man who graduate with honors from University of Dirty Tricks. "We just got you out in time!" he say, proud like rooster who think sun come up because of his singing.

I turn to him with eyes like angry eagle, "Yes, and you get me IN there just in time also!"

"Don't try to be big hero again - I know what happened! Ballsak was your problem, so you make me his problem, so he become your problem again, so you can be SuperFuckWit saving me from problem you create! Very clever, like fox who burn down henhouse then want medal for saving one chicken!"

Clitter stare at me with eyes big like sheep seeing wolf wearing shepherd clothes. He know I see through him. My eyes become like eyes of Azhdaha, desert serpent god who can see through mountains and into people's lying hearts.

"What you say about that?!" I scream like banshee with megaphone. Nurse come running in, thinking maybe patient gone crazy from too much hospital food. But Clitter already shrinking like balloon meeting angry porcupine as he backs away through door.

Nurse tells me get some rest, but how can rest when truth more twisted than imam's Friday sermon? Sometimes in life, winning feel exactly like losing, except you also must smile and say thank you.

CHAPTER 33

Back to my Bush

Hospital throws me out after 24 hours, like unwanted cabbage roll at village feast. They give me paper saying "Please to stop taking drugs." Ha! Like I had choice when Alboscum tie me down and make me human pin cushion!

But no - Clitter pigdog not tell them real story. Why would he? Official story much better for his shiny police record: "Stupid Kazakh girl Lapshagul becomes junkie and trades favors with Albanians for bad drugs." Because obviously, what else I do in magical UK except sell body parts and live fantasy rockstar life? Just another dirty immigrant trying to steal English tea and crumpets!

Clitwit write this version in his fancy reports, keep his ass clean like Queen's China while he gets medal for catching Albos. He use me like goat tied to tree to catch tiger, then throw me away like yesterday's borscht.

I wobble down empty streets, I wobble down empty streets, wind biting worse than camel with three teeth. Everything hurts in places that make me want to cry to Allah himself. Nose running like spring mountain stream, skin wet like clams in market.

And worst? My body screaming for whatever poison Albos put in me - congratulations, Lapshagul, you now proper London junkie! I catch sight in shop window - Jesus Mary Mohammed! Is that ghost of dead prostitute? No, just me in torn jacket, no shoes, only stupid hospital slippers that look like something cat would bury in litterbox. No phone, no money, just shame and addiction for company.

Trek to Elephant Castle like punishment march in army, but surprise! Can't get in flat because police tape everywhere and new locks. So where does homeless junkie Lapshagul go? Like lost dog, I follow nose to Bush.

"LAPPY!!!" Landlordlady screams when she sees me, crushing me in a hug that could squeeze vodka from a potato. She smells of discount perfume that even a market stall wouldn't sell, but her giant brown arms are the safest place in London right now.

It wasn't always like this. Last time, she kicked me out like stray dog, cursed my name, said I brought nothing but trouble. But London changes people fast. Maybe she heard what happened— how I was left for dead, how I clawed my way back. Or maybe she just missed me.

Either way, when she sees me now, there's no anger, no suspicion. Just relief.

Then she stops and looks at me with eyes that see straight through bullshit into soul. She knows. She always knows.

She carries me inside and run bath that steam up windows like sauna in Moscow (not that I ever been). Then - this part bit weird but nice weird - she wash me like I'm her own child. Her hands soft like steppe grass but strong like grandmother making bread dough and for first time since hospital, I feel human again.

After bath, she wrap me in towels big enough for circus tent, carry me upstairs to my old room. Thank Allah room still empty - maybe even He feel sorry for poor Lapshagul? Room smell of lavender, not fear and regret like hospital.

Then comes massage that make Russian army training feel like butterfly kiss. Her hands declare war on every muscle that dare be tense.

Sometimes pleasure, sometimes pain, like life in London - you never know which one coming next. She leave to get pajamas, and I lay there, feeling like piece of meat that been tenderized with love hammer.

I stretch, look out window into growing dark and... BLYAD! There he is! Bernard! Little bald head bouncing like ping-pong ball. I jump up, naked as truth, and scream, "You fucking pig's twat Bernard!"

I climb out window onto roof, cold air biting my everything, but Bernard disappear like ghost in morning sun. Was he real? Or maybe Albo drugs make me see things? Maybe brain now more scrambled than breakfast at greasy spoon cafe?

So there I stand, on roof, naked, freezing, staring at empty room through window. Landlordlady yell from behind like angry mother hen, "Lappy, what devil got into you? Get back inside!" I obey, put on tracksuit and clean knickers she brings, but keep watching that window. Either Bernard real and playing games, or I go crazy. In London, both equally possible.

So here I am, once again sprawled on tiny bed in tiny room at top of tiny house in the Bush, thinking what absolute circus-show my life become in last two months. Back to beginning, yes? Ha! Not quite beginning - more like basement of beginning. No money, no phone, no fancy clothes, but maybe... maybe I have something else now.

Brain starts getting fuzzy and dreams are circling like hungry wolves - you know, like when Uncle Nurlan throw sheep guts to them for festival game in village, except I'm sheep guts. Dreams want to play with me tonight, but I'm not sure if I want playful dreams or just black nothing- sleep.

What I get instead is crazy mix - like DJ in bad London club, switching between awake-not-awake, then tumbling through memories of people I know, people I wish I didn't know, then soft darkness like inside of rich person's coffin (not that I've been in one, but I imagine very fancy), then back again, round and round like broken carousel.

Morning comes with sunshine so bright it hurt eyes like police flashlight, and there's Landlordlady hovering over me, holding tea and what she calls 'Jamaican toast' - still don't understand why Jamaica need special toast, but okay. My face does something weird... oh yes, remembering now - is thing called 'smile'. Been while since face do that trick.

"Got a visitor for you," she say, and before I can ask who want to see poor Kazakh girl this early, in walks ClitWit, looking like toy soldier with his shiny buttons. For once, I don't want to make joke about his name.

"Looking very official today, Dickie," I say, trying to be nice instead of usual sarcastic self. He hold big plastic bag like he Father Christmas from Scotland Yard.

"I've got your things," he say, showing me stuff from flat in Elephant's Castle - my phone, passport with visa that running out faster than toilet paper in dodgy pub. But money? Poof! Gone like magic trick. "Evidence against Albanians," he explain. "They going to prison for slavery and money laundering. But first, need your statement. Please." This 'please' at end make me almost trust him. Almost.

Landlordlady still there, putting her big nose in business like true British person. "Listen here, Lappy," she say, all wisdom of East London in her voice, "You do what PC Clitter is asking, yeah? Otherwise, these bad men will go free and do same thing to other girls. That'd be on your conscience, innit?"

First thought in head is 'mind own business, big mama', but then thinking maybe she right. Maybe time to listen to people who actually follow rules in this crazy place.

"Right then, I've said my piece," Landlordlady announce like queen finishing speech, and waddles out.

Clitter says we going to police station, so I put on clothes, check phone - everybody and their dog send message while I gone - and tuck passport in pocket like precious thing it is. "Where my kamcha?" I ask, missing my whip like missing old friend.

"That nasty whip? Evidence now. Matches all the marks on your body from hospital photos." Then he tell me about doctors examining me while I knocked out cold, and my eyes go wide like saucers. Thinking to self: they doing proper job here, maybe smart to play nice, follow rules for change.

Tell Clitter about having no money (true story), and suddenly he giving me £500 from police secret money pot. Must sign paper - official now, I'm proper snitch, grass, whatever English call person who talk to police. Blyad!

He asks about cameras in flat, and I just blame Albanians - make him happy like kid with ice cream. He wants Ballsak in jail long time anyway, and better if I stay useful for future, sneaky little desert rat that he is.

"What about visa?" I ask, worried about getting kicked back to steppes.

"No problem," he say, proud like puffed poser. "You're a witness in a big Crown Court case now. No deportation."

Everything fixed neat and tidy, like bow on present. High five! (Is what Americans say, yes? I learn).

CHAPTER 34

Respect?

So here I am, thinking like stupid village girl that I can put all the shitstorm from last months behind me and become proper London lady. Look at me now - friend with policeman (only one, but still counts), got papers that make me legal person (mostly), and soon getting benefits that will pay rent to Landlordlady who probably thinks I'm prostitute but takes money anyway. Maybe even get job where I don't have to explain three times that "Would you like fries with that?" is not sexual invitation.

My English getting better too - now I only sound like Borat's cousin who went to community college, not complete village idiot who learned English from porn movies and BBC nature shows. What was I thinking, trying to be Kazakh Queen of London? Stupid like trying to milk bull - lots of pulling, no results.

On phone with Mfanni now, trying to make nice-nice, but must keep mouth shut about Clitter business and witness statement against Alboscum.

Trust? In London? Is like trying to find virgin in brothel - maybe exists but probably lying. Everyone here working angle sharper than mother's best kitchen knife. Took me time, but now I understand - London is not city, is jungle where snakes wear designer clothes and backstab with expensive phones.

Need a drink bad. And food. And someone to talk to who won't try to kill me (at least not today). Mfanni is only option - like choosing between getting kick in face or kick in ass.

We meet at Flying Tishkan, because where else can two semi-legal immigrants go to drink overpriced bozo and pretend we're sophisticated?

"Bernard?" she asks, mouth full of cheap booze. "You seen him?"

"Think saw him through window once," I tell her, "But probably just hallucination, like when grandmother ate wrong mushrooms and thought teakettle was government spy."

She tells me Bernard scared of me, hiding. I tell her he better hide good, because when I find that little rat-faced traitor, I'm going to make his balls into earrings. She laughs so hard, bozo comes out nose like fountain in rich person's garden. Fake Kazakh-Russian boys cleaning up mess look at us like we just escaped from mental hospital for dangerous immigrants.

But universe has funny way of making jokes, yes? Just when thinking life might be normal, door explodes open and in walks two more Alboscum who make previous look like baby rabbits. One waves a gun, other one - size of small house with face that looks like it was carved from angry potato - comes straight for me.

Me and Mfanni sit there like two chickens who just realized they're at KFC. This is moment when all those nice thoughts about becoming respectable citizen turn into laugh track in bad sitcom. London teaching me same lesson again and again - just when think you climbing out of shithole, someone comes along with bigger shovel.

But wait! Life has more surprises than babushka's mystery stew! Because who appears like magic? Bernard! Little perverted Bernard who once asked me to dress as milkmaid and spank him with wooden spoon- now suddenly ninja assassin!

One minute giant Alboscum breathing down neck like angry bull, next minute - knife in throat, blood spraying across restaurant like garden sprinkler! Borscht and beshmarmak on table now wearing new sauce - not the kind you want to taste! Poor baursak sitting there soaking up evidence like guilty sponge. All courtesy of man who cries during cat food commercials!

Body hits floor with thud, while traditional Kazakh feast gets very untraditional new garnish. Other Alboscum runs away like village drunk who spot angry wife with rolling pin. Even fake-Kazakh waiters looking green - probably first time they see real Kazakh-style dinner entertainment!

So much for respect and normal life. Past keeps following me like hungry dog after meat truck. When will it stop? Probably when hell freezes over and devil starts selling ice cream. Welcome to London, darling - where even happy endings come with side of violence and confusion.

CHAPTER 35

The Common Denominator

After police business at Flying Tishkan (and Bernard doing his sneaky- sneaky private chat with big boss policeman around corner), three of us go back to my room in Bush House.

My brilliant idea! Not even late, and look - we get vodka on way! Me and Mfanni doing giggle-whispers like silly schoolgirls, saying how maybe- maybe Bernard gets lucky tonight with two pretty ladies, yes? After all, this strange little man just save us from very painful death. Respect due, as London people say!

First bottle goes bye-bye and Mfanni's tongue starts playing hopscotch with words: 'Bernaaaard... listen-listen... you sssneaky bastard... you're the one... the one what makes all this... this... this MESS make... wait- wait... you're the common... common... hiccup... DENOMINATOR! Ha! Big word for sneaky man, innit?'

I scratch head like monkey looking at iPhone. "What is this common dominator business?"

Mfanni waves finger like professor giving lecture: "Use your brain, Lappy! He's always there, yeah? When shit hits the fan, Bernard is lurking like a cockroach! He is a trouble magnet, this one!"

Ah! Common denominator! I add this clever phrase to my special English words collection. The always-there man, the one who brings chaos like birthday present - this is common denominator. Like bad penny, but smaller and more annoying.

I look at Bernard, who now resembles sad puppy on floor, vodka making his brain go mushy-mushy. Me and Mfanni sit on bed like proper queens of England, looking down at our little subject. "So, Bernard, what you say? You are this common denominator, yes-no?"

He says nothing, just wobbles like jelly in earthquake. Not looking so clever now - not big KGB spy man, not James Bond with fancy watch, not ninja warrior of death. No, Bernard is just silly little pervert man who attracts trouble like honey attracts bears.

"Too bad you forget your mouse costume, Bernard," I say with maximum cheekiness. "Could have done special cheese dance for you!" Me and Mfanni laugh like hyenas at zoo feeding time.

Bernard sits still like clever fish - ah, he learns! But then Mfanni pulls out special cigarette that makes room smell funny. I say no-no because good Kazakh girl never does drugs (ha!), but now everything gets bit crazy.

Mfanni decides to do special London dance show - bazookas flying everywhere like they have own passport and visa. "Hey Bernie baby, like what you see?" she shouts like market seller with fresh fish. But Bernard keeps face straight like English guard at palace.

Then brilliant idea hits my vodka-brain! Time for special Kazakh tradition – famous Golden Fountain of Steppe! I pull down pants, turn around like ballet dancer, and... BLYAT! Big mistake! Bernard sitting near electric fire with loose wires! My golden blessing hits socket, and ZAP! - electricity runs up body like angry snake! Me and Bernard both get shock like woman who lift carpet to shake dust but find whole family sitting under it drinking tea!"

I screech, and Bernard jumps up - then down he goes, flat like pancake! Mfanni laughing so hard her chocolate bazookas doing whole dance routine by themselves. But then... silence comes, heavy as stone.

As we try to wake him, Bernard suddenly mumbles, barely audible. His eyes jumping around like drunk fireflies at village festival. "You never got it, did you, Lappy? You think you're just surviving... but all this? All of us?" He gives a small laugh, like he's finally understood some private joke. Then his eyes close, a cryptic smile flickering across his face.

Bernard now not moving. We poke-poke, shake-shake, even try traditional Kazakh wake-up kick. Nothing. Bernard gone to big spy meeting in sky. Me standing with wet pants around ankles (very dignified, yes?), world spinning faster than gossip in village hair salon.

Mfanni whispers like she passing code through prison wall: "Lowest common denominator now, Bernard. Lowest common denominator."

My eyes start doing emergency meeting with brain - they point to window, to flat roof outside. Aha! Sometimes best plan is plan that comes when no other choice, yes? I climb on bed, open window, Mfanni confused.

Now comes fun part - moving Bernard! He heavy like wet carpet! I grab collar, pull-pull, but body just flops. "Hey!" I whisper-shout to Mfanni, "Help me with this potato sack of trouble!"

We pull together like donkeys pulling broken cart up mountain, but window decides to play silly game - SLAM! Gets stuck halfway! And now, cherry on top of problem cake, Landlordlady doing angry knock-knock concert on door: "Wot's all that racket about then?!"

Bernard's body makes final journey through window with sound effects like broken bagpipe - wheeze-fart-plop! His phone falls out - quick thinking, I grab and hide in special pocket of panties. Very James Bond, yes?

We jump back inside, close window as if nothing happen. Open door to angry Landlordlady who storms in like bull who smell red flag. But then - her nose better than police dog!

Smells Mfanni's special cigarette!

"Drug taking in my 'ouse?!" she screams like tea kettle on fire. "Get out! Both of you! Before the nick comes sniffing!" She throws us out, my things trailing behind me like sad parade.

Five minutes later, me and Mfanni sitting on cold London pavement. She offers room at her place, but brain is doing clever calculations. When Landlordlady finds Bernard doing sunbathing forever on roof, police will come. They will look at me first - always look at foreign girl first, yes?

Only way out is to blame Mfanni (sorry, friend, but survival is survival).

So I pick up bags, wave goodbye to Mfanni who still giggling like she watching funny cat video, and run to find taxi. Sometimes best friend is no friend, especially when dead Bernard on roof and police getting ready to play detective games.

CHAPTER 36

The Scorpion's Tail

'Saiqymazaqtyñ äpkesi qaıda?'

The accent is so thick it makes my brain hurt like bad hangover, and I'm pretending not to understand even though words are swimming in my head clear as vodka. I'm answering Bernard's phone, which is buzzing against my lady parts because that's where I stashed it (don't judge - you try finding good pocket in women's jeans in London).

Again: 'Saiqymazaqtyñ äpkesi qaıda?'

I wait for different words, maybe nice English hello or even Russian curse word, but no - just more Kazakh from someone who learned it from textbook. They're asking where clown's sister is, which is funny because that's me, though right now I'm not feeling very ha-ha.

Now standing outside some budget hotel that probably hasn't seen vacuum cleaner since Margaret Thatcher was boss lady of England. Was about to check in when mystery caller with hidden number made Bernard's phone do happy dance in my pants.

Now I'm paranoid, looking everywhere like tourist who lost passport. I'm searching for giant scorpion tail that my imagination says is going to kebab me any second. My brain is working about as well as frozen calculator - which is to say, not at all.

Caller gives up, phone goes quiet. I stuff it back in secret phone pocket (aka panties) and drag myself into hotel that smells like wet dog and old people. Lying on bed, I keep waiting for shoe to drop (learned from BBC detective show - British people very serious about gravity, I think).

It hit me then, only thing make sense! Bernard (speaking perfect Kazakh), Mfanni (always disappearing before trouble), Vertigo (changing from street pimp to businessman overnight), Landlordlady (love me then hate me then love me), Clitter (appearing exactly when needed, like magical policeman) - they're all just pieces of big nasty scorpion puzzle. While I've been thinking I'm smart girl living London adventure, they've been playing me like cheap balalaika. I've been too busy admiring my own cleverness to see giant arachnid death trap dancing above my head.

'Saiqymazaqtyñ äpkesi qaıda?' The words bounce around my skull like ping-pong ball as I drift into sleep that's jumpier than newspaper on windy day.

Truth is, being clown's sister was supposed to be my golden ticket. Back home, I told family, "Soon everyone will say 'Sister of the Clown' like it's fancy title, like Queen of England or Winner of British Bake Off!" They worried it would bring shame and police trouble, but I was too busy dreaming of fame to listen. Now here I am, on plastic bed that squeaks like old Soviet elevator, in hotel that TripAdvisor forgot.

Bernard's phone buzzes again. New voice, speaking English this time: "Where is she? Come on, I need information, or this will end badly for you!" I know this voice - belongs to Clitter, London's grumpiest policeman. I hang up faster than kebab shop closes at prayer time.

Then my own phone starts dancing. It's Clitter again, but he doesn't know I've got Bernard's phone - ha! Small victory, like finding extra fry at bottom of McDonald's bag. "Hello Officer Clitter," I say in my poshest English, "How absolutely splendid to hear from you!"

What follows is most racist rant I've heard since Uncle Bakhit got drunk at wedding and started talking about Russians. Clitter goes full steam ahead about immigrants and liberals until I can't help but poke angry bear: "Officer Clitty-Clot, you are corrupt like Kazakh traffic cop - but at least they honest about taking bribes!"

Bad move. Very bad move. Like poking angry bear with stick made of sausages. Now he's threatening me with revenge bigger than my mama's wedding feast. I try to backtrack, but he's gone, leaving me alone with my panic and imagination that's working overtime like illegal sweatshop.

The scorpion in my head is doing full assembly now, like IKEA furniture but with more poison. Every enemy I've made is becoming part of its body - Clitter, Ballsak, Landlordlady, Vertigo, Abdul, the Lord, the Minister - all morphing into black shiny pieces of doom-bug

As head spins, I'm thinking maybe London adventure not so fun anymore. Maybe should have stayed home and married cousin Nurlan who smells like armpit but at least doesn't try to murder me with scorpion metaphors.

Bernard's phone still going crazy, buzz-buzz like angry bee having epileptic fit. And whole time I'm getting this feeling, like when babushka used to say she could feel storm coming in her knee - except feeling is in my head, not knee, and storm is already here, just nobody else knows yet.

I'm staring at phone like it's magical fortune-telling device from ancient Kazakhstan (we don't have these, by way - just regular phones that sometimes work when weather is good). My eyes probably look like owls we have back home, except owls usually more intelligent than me right now.

But wait! Something clicking in brain like when you finally

143

understand why British people say "bloody hell" even when nothing bleeding...

BAM! Like getting hit by London bus, idea smashes into my head like beautiful Soviet-era construction project - except hopefully not falling apart so quick.

So once again, I book table at Flying Tishkan for five. Why five? Don't ask - sometimes best plans in life like taxi driver's shortcut: makes no sense, but somehow works.

Then get cab (driver only try to scam me little bit this time), walk into Flying Tishkan like I own place (I don't - thank God, too much paperwork), talk to Arsen who say okay because he scared of me now (good strategy in London - make people little bit scared, they always say okay).

Then clever part come - I leave Bernard's phone under table like little present from spy school and go sit in pub across street, and watch Flying Tishkan like KGB agent, except with less fancy equipment and more confusion about British weather.

Everything going according to plan - Clitter and police buddies show up (looking very important, like roosters at government parade - not like police back home who sometimes must push own vehicle). Then big black car arrives with three guys who look like they eat small countries for breakfast - must be Alboscum boys. Who leak information? Universe full of leaky things in London.

Then Mfanni make appearance and - holy borscht! - even Vertigo shows up, fresh from prison looking like he had holiday at British spa! In my country, prison make you look like you live in basement for three generations. Here, look like you just finish yoga retreat.

Everything coming together like perfect storm, except storm in Britain usually just mean little rain and everyone panic buying tea. But this storm? This storm going to be proper Kazakh-style storm, and I sitting here in pub, watching it all start, thinking maybe I not so stupid tourist anymore. Maybe I become proper London creature - half scared, half excited, 110% crazy.

CHAPTER 37

The Dinner Party

Ha! Look at this – everyone's here now! Some came because I invited them (how stupid can they be), others are hunting for Bernard, and the rest? Oh, they just want to find who killed Bernard. Very popular man suddenly, no? Clitter's boys must have found Bernard's phone under table – probably next to last week's chewing gum – because now my phone buzzes with ClitHeads's number. Smart bastard figured it out.

Give him cookie!

But wait minute – who is real puppet master here? Who is pulling strings? To find this sneaky rat, I must look at whole picture, like taxman searching for missing ten tenge.

All threads leading back to Bernard, this I know like smell of burning cabbage. He's been hanging around me since beginning, always there with his sweaty hands and suspicious phone calls. But... but Bernard not smart enough to be mastermind. Even with his precious Kazakh princess of London making his little bald head spin, and his weird obsession with me, something bigger must be pushing him. Who made him dance like drunk bear at Russian circus?

Across street, they wait for me like wolves outside chicken house. I know whatever they planning probably involve lots of sharp objects and zero hugs, so should probably – what's English saying? – get my arse in gear bloody quick. But I'm stuck like frozen pelmeni because where do I run? First need answer-who pulling Bernard strings while he pulls everyone else's?

Clock going tick-tick-tick like time bomb in my head, and soon whole Tishkan crew will pour onto street like angry ants whose hill just got kicked. Still can't move – body refusing orders like stubborn Soviet bureaucrat. I close eyes and cry but tears not mine – they belong to a green-eyed boy I left behind, thinking I become big success in London. Ha! Instead, become professional mess – part-time whore, full-time blackmailer, and now apparently murder expert! Mother would be so proud, yes?

Then – BOOM! – like lightning hitting vodka factory, truth hits me. Not Kazakh spies behind this, not fancy crime lords, not even my bastard ex- husband who probably still angry I set his tracksuit collection on fire. No, no, no – want to know who really controlling Bernard and others? ME!

I have big sign floating over head saying, "Please Exploit Me – Free Samples!" like cheap perfume store in Oxford Street. Bernard, Clitter, Mfanni, Vertigo – they all pull my strings because I basically hand them puppet controller with instruction manual!

Now I sit here in pub that make Soviet-era toilet look fancy, while they wait in restaurant smelling of kumis and broken dreams. They sharpen knives and probably practicing evil laughs. I feel empty.

What now, eh? Stay and fight like angry babushka defending last cabbage roll? Or run away like cockroach when kitchen light comes on? Only one option really – go back to place I never wanted to see again, where all started and figure out how I got here in first place.

We all know where that is, yes? (Hint: starts with 'K', ends with 'azakhstan', and middle part still terrible!)

APPENDIX I

A Humorous Guide to Places,
Terms, and Cultural References

Places

Kazakhstan & Central Asia

Almaty
A city that thinks being an ex-capital is cooler than being a current one.

Astana
A city where architecture looks like an architect lost a bet with the universe.

Betpak-Dala
A desert so desolate that camels pack extra camels just in case, leading to an infinite recursion of backup humps.

Caspian Sea
The only body of water that's technically single but has five clingy exes (countries) who won't stop arguing over who gets to keep what after the breakup.

Tian Shan
A mountain range so impressive that other mountain ranges have posters of it on their bedroom walls.

Tomenaryk
A place so remote that even Google Maps asks "Are you sure?" when you search for it.

Zhanakorgan
The location where Marco Polo allegedly stopped and said "Okay, maybe I've gone far enough east."

United Kingdom & London

Bedlam
The only asylum that became a tourist attraction and then a nightclub- proving that London never really changes.

Belgravia
The only place in London where having just one butler is considered "going through a rough patch."

Bond Street
Where tourists come to understand why their travel insurance specifically excluded "shopping-induced cardiac events."

Buckingham Palace
The only place where working from home requires parliamentary approval and a ceremonial trumpet fanfare.

Cockfosters
A location specifically designed to make American tourists giggle while reading the tube map.

Elephant and Castle
The only place in London named after what sounds like a rejected medieval chess piece but is actually a pub that nobody can find anymore.

Glastonbury
A festival where the queue for the toilets are longer than most headliners careers.

Hackney
Where your rent doubles every time someone opens a vegan cafe.

Hammersmith
The neighborhood that turned a massive concrete flyover into a tourist attraction by convincing everyone it's "architectural character."

Knightsbridge
If your idea of fun is stepping on small dogs owned by rich women while dodging Lamborghinis, welcome.

Mayfair
A district so exclusive that even GPS systems ask for your bank statement before providing directions.

Oxford Street
A gladiator arena where the strongest tourists battle for cheap handbags and overpriced sneakers.

Shepherds Bush
Despite the name, neither shepherds nor bushes have been spotted here in decades. Mostly pigeons and people regretting their life choices.

Soho
A neighborhood where "quiet night out" is considered an oxymoron and sleep is just a suggestion between parties.

Trafalgar Square

The only place in London where pigeons have successfully established their own parliament, with better attendance records than Westminster.

Zone 1-London
An area where standing still on the wrong side of the escalator is considered a more serious crime than actual crimes.

Zone 6-London
The land where "I live in London" requires a 20-minute explanation involving train timetables and defensive justifications.

Other international locations

Albania
A country that decided mountains, beaches, and bunkers were the perfect threesome.

Cosmos Hotel
Moscow's middle finger to both gravity and Western hotel aesthetics.

Kingston
The only capital city where showing up three hours late makes you suspiciously early.

Siberia
The only place where "it's a dry cold" is both a weather report and a cry for help.

Food & Drinks

Baursak
A traditional form of self-sabotage where you promise to eat 'just one more' approximately 47 times until your stomach feels like a yurt full of wrestlers.

Beshbarmak
The dish that proves Kazakhs really love eating horses, even if the rest of the world finds it concerning.

Borscht
The soup that made an entire region debate whether it's Ukrainian or Russian, but let's be honest, nobody actually likes it sober.

Bozo
Fermented miracle: conversation starter, truth serum, and potential biological weapon of mass destruction.

Crumpet
The only breakfast item that makes you feel posh while essentially eating an edible kitchen sponge.

Earl Grey
British tea that makes people pretend they have refined tastes, but deep

down, they all want coffee.

Kebab
The evolutionary missing link between a respectable dinner and your 3 AM life choices.

Kespe
The ancient practice of attempting to convince visitors that your irregularly cut noodles are "artisanal" and "deliberately rustic."

Kumis
What happens when milk decides to join a nomadic motorcycle gang.

Kurt
Traditional dried cheese balls that are harder than your ex's heart and twice as salty.

Lapsha
When your mouth is cooking up more noodles than your kitchen. The only dish that's served best directly to your ears.

Pelmeni
A food that requires you to have a philosophical debate about the nature of dumplings while folding them at precisely the right speed.

PG Tips
The liquid courage behind every British passive-aggressive note about washing up the mugs.

Raki
Side effects may include thinking you can dance and temporary fluency in Ancient Greek.

Samruk cognac
A sacred bird's way of saying "let's get unsacred".

Shashlyk
The only food that can turn tough meat into a delicacy and drunk uncles into philosophers.

Shirchay
Central Asia's way of showing that tea can be both breakfast and a full day's allowance of sodium and fat.

Shorpo
Traditional Kazakh soup, usually served with extra bones, floating mystery objects, and unsolicited life advice from your grandmother.

Shubat
The drink that convinces tourists they're brave until they actually try it, then convinces locals they're hilarious.

Yorkshire Pudding
The only food that can simultaneously be a complete failure and absolutely perfect depending on which British grandmother you ask.

Zhaya

The only meat that can make you feel guilty for eating it because the horse probably had a better pedigree than you.

Cultural Items & Traditions

Babushka
A sweet old lady who will spoil you endlessly but also curse in ways that shake the heavens.

Bederi
The are of making things fancy when plain would have worked just fine.

Besik taspa
Kazakh parents' first lesson in securing cargo before a long journey.

Bilezik
Proof that humans will wear anything shiny enough to impress grandmothers and pickpockets.

Chapan
The original power suit of the Silk Road, with more pockets than your life has problems.

Cossak
A person whose idea of formal wear includes more ammunition than buttons

Dauylpaz
A traditional way of letting everyone within a five-mile radius know you're feeling dramatic.

Dombra
A two-stringed instrument that, like your ex, only knows two emotions but somehow still manages to make you cry.

Gul
The suffix that turns any name into a bouquet.

Jezökşe
The reason some men suddenly become very generous.

Kamcha
The only whip that doubles as a family heirloom and fashion statement.

Kara-Zhorga
The only dance where your arms and legs do different things, but somehow it still looks cool.

Kazan
The Central Asian infinity pot—no matter how much you cook in it, there's always enough for one more guest.

Kyrgyz Circus
Where "bareback riding" means "standing on horse while shooting arrows."

Matryoshka Dolls

Proof that even toys in Russia come with existential crises: "What if I'm just another doll inside a bigger doll?"

Nauryz
A celebration that proves Central Asians knew about spring cleaning before Marie Kondo.

Qazaq Kuresi
The Kazakh martial art where two people try to make each other eat dirt while wearing fancy bathrobes.

Steppe
Earth's greatest screensaver: grass to infinity.

Taban
The part of your body that only remembers it exists when it hits furniture.

Yurt
A mobile home for nomads who were into glamping before it was cool.

Zhaushy
Traditional matchmaker who's basically Tinder without the swiping, but with 100% more judgment.

People & Historical Figures

Aigul Kossanova
If you don't know her, just nod and pretend you do. It's safer that way.

Gary Lineker
The man who made Match of the Day must-see TV by not showing up.

Genghis Khan
History's most successful family planning enthusiast.

Hugh Grant
The British actor who has played the same awkwardly charming character for 30 years and still gets away with it.

Josef Stalin
Transformed "comrade" from friendly greeting to last words.

Kate Middleton
Future Queen of England and full-time professional smiler.

Margaret Thatcher
PM who snatched milk from kids but gave bankers champagne.
Mother Therese

Mother Theresa
Proof that passive-aggressive kindness can change the world.

Vladimir Lenin
A statue that spent more time pointing at nothing than actually leading.

Willie Wonka
A candymaker who believes that child endangerment is an acceptable quality control method.

Slang & Expressions

Bozhe moy
Russian for "Oh my God," most often used after looking at London rent prices.

Findom
A wild subculture where people willingly give their money to a stranger just for fun.

Goolies
The real-life reset button that no man ever wants pressed.

Innit
London's way of asking for confirmation while demanding agreement.

Kynap
A Russian who wears a shapan over his Adidas tracksuit for Kazakh authenticity.

Nunu
A term of endearment, unless said with an evil tone, in which case you should run.

Prozzies
The reason some men suddenly believe in supporting small businesses.

Pussyclat
A Caribbean insult that sounds funny but is actually very rude.

Shagging
A temporary escape from reality, usually followed by regret or breakfast.

Todger
A biological compass that only points toward bad decisions.

Brands, Media & Consumer Goods

Botox
Expensive paralysis for the professionally insecure.

Daily Mail
The newspaper that believes everything is the fault of immigrants, the EU, or Meghan Markle.

Fairy Liquid
The soap that makes dishes cleaner than your conscience.

Gucci
Designer clothing for people who hate money and love logos.

Harrods
A museum of overpriced everything with a food court.

Lidl
Cheaper than Tesco, and twice as likely to sell you something expired.

Плейбой Россия
Magazine that makes both communists and capitalists uncomfortable.

Radio Eurasia
Soviet CNN with extra static.

Stoli
Russia's liquid courage, now with extra geopolitical tension.

Tesco
Where Britain's lower middle class goes to argue with self-checkouts.

Technology & Apps

Google Maps
The digital assistant that thinks U-turns are a lifestyle choice.

GPS
Your mom's voice but with more "recalculating."

Grindr
A digital advent calendar where every window opens to an eggplant emoji.

Tinder
Where "entrepreneur" means they're between jobs and own a cryptocurrency.

Trip Advisor
A magical realm where a single hair can spark a 500-word review.

Miscellaneous & Mythology

Albasty
History's deadliest cosmetologist.

Azhdaha
The geological equivalent of "you wouldn't like me when I'm angry."

Brexit
The political equivalent of drunk texting "we're done" to Europe.

Ferret

A slinky that grew fur and chose chaos.

Gulag
Soviet vacation camp, but with extra suffering.

Jerboa
The desert's answer to "what if we gave a rat springs?"

Marmot
A groundhog that chose violence as a lifestyle.

Oligarch
Russian billionaire who "earned" his money totally legally. Definitely.

Ouroboros
The cosmic symbol for "I told you it would come back to bite you."

Pidjondar
Like "pigeon" but with more existential dread.

Samovar
A kettle that decided to become architecture.

Shaitan
Like your mother-in-law, but older and more judgy about clay people.

Suluk
Like a bad relative, but smaller and more honest about wanting your blood.

Tobet
The steppe's original "find out" after someone's "fuck around."

Tyshkan
A tiny philosopher who believes all of life's problems can be solved with cheese.

Yak
A buffalo that discovered hair conditioner.

ABOUT THE AUTHOR

Gul Aina

Gul Aina is a Kazakh-born writer, satirist, and healthcare professional living in London. A decade ago, she fled Kazakhstan for political reasons, seeking refuge in the UK, where she rebuilt her life while navigating the eccentricities of British culture. When she's not writing, she continues her work in healthcare, a profession she first trained for in her homeland.

Her writing is a sharp, unfiltered, and often hilarious reflection of her own journey as an outsider trying to make sense of a new world. Drawing from real-life experiences, Gul Aina infuses her storytelling with biting humor, cultural observations, and a fearless critique of power structures—both in the West and within the Kazakh diaspora.

Her debut novel introduces Lapshugal, a bold and unapologetic Kazakh woman making her way through London's chaos with wit, survival instincts, and a knack for getting into (and out of) trouble. Gul Aina is currently working on two follow-up books: an origin story of Lapshugal, tracing her path from Kazakhstan to London, and a sequel that plunges her into the hidden world of the elite and powerful figures within the Kazakh diaspora—where money, influence, and scandal go hand in hand.

Gul Aina writes to entertain, to expose, and to give voice to the absurdities of exile, identity, and ambition. Through her sharp satire, she turns survival into an art form and hardship into comedy and poignant counterpoint.

You can follow her work and updates on upcoming releases at Facebook, Twitter and Instagram.

www.ingramcontent.com/pod-product-compliance
Lightning Source LLC
Chambersburg PA
CBHW060225180626
46813CB00007B/2960